ALPHA MOUNTAIN: HERO

BOOK 1

VANESSA VALE

RENEE ROSE

Alpha Mountain: Hero

Cover design: Bridger Media

Cover graphic: Deposit Photos: Fourleaflovers, appalachianview

ALPHA MOUNTAIN: HERO

A Mountain Man Mercenary Romance

She's my best friend's sister. Off-limits.
Before he died, I promised I'd never touch her.
After years in the military, I'm back in Montana
determined to clear his name.
A mercenary set on revenge. No one's hero—just a
mountain man.
Now, I owe it to my friend to protect his sister.
Except being near her shreds my resolve. She tempts
me at every turn.
Each day is a brutal torment, and my honor and
willpower
...are about to snap.

Welcome to Alpha Mountain, the powerful new series by USA Today bestselling authors Vanessa Vale and Renee Rose. Where strong, alpha men will move mountains to protect and claim their women.

PROLOGUE

FORD

BUCK and I carried the empty keg between us.

Here in Sparks, there was no war. No enemy. The only chance of being killed tonight was from alcohol poisoning or getting eaten by a bear.

We were used to moving around under the cover of darkness, but that was to evade the enemy, not to cut across a field beneath a Montana black night sky.

Neither of us had been home for over sixteen months, and I'd forgotten how dark it got. No big cities anywhere nearby. No desert either. We weren't wearing our fatigues, and we weren't carrying multiple weapons.

"Did you hear Lee Landers is taking over his dad's mechanic shop?" Buck asked.

"I know. The most exotic thing he'll see of the world is the undercarriage of a sixty-seven GTO." I took a deep breath.

Fuck, I missed that scent. The tang of pine and damp earth was as much a reminder of home as Gram and Gramps. Or the twenty or so friends from high school who had just finished off this keg, listening to music, fooling around and having fun in the back forty behind us.

"The *undercarriage* I want to see is that of Kenzie Michelson. She was hot in high school, but did you see her tonight? Were her tits always that big?" Buck held up his hands to show how big he thought they were as he grinned.

"Why the hell are you helping me carry this keg when you could be helping Kenzie out of her panties?"

Our long legs ate up the distance between the party and the truck. The get-together was in the usual party spot by the creek, originally chosen so my grandparents wouldn't know about any of the late night get-togethers. Of course, I'd been stupid to think that. They'd been pissed back in the day when they'd learned of them, but now? I was twenty-three.

I'd had hair on my balls for years, but I'd also become a SEAL and gone to war. Neither of them gave a shit if I wanted to get drunk with a few old friends. Hell, they were content I was in one piece. And home.

They were off on a trip to a nearby casino for two nights, having their own kind of good time.

"She's not port pussy," Buck countered, stopping when we got to the truck. He leaned against the back end. "Still, I get the feeling she wants me to be her ride out of town."

I remembered Kenzie, big tits and all. I'd been cautious where I stuck my dick in high school because I had plans. Plans that didn't involve a surprise baby and wife at eighteen. I'd wanted out of Sparks, to follow in Gramps' footsteps in the military. So I understood where Buck was coming from. We both might be up for a fun fuck but nothing more than that.

I pulled down the tailgate and jumped into the bed. Fuck, I loved this truck. I'd bought it when I was sixteen after spending the summer working at the seed and feed lugging sacks of grain, bales of hay and every other piece of heavy farming shit. It'd helped me get into shape for basic training and eventually BUD/S.

That had been hell, but I had Buck to tell me to stop being a pussy whenever I had an inkling of quitting. Now it seemed I had to give him a pep talk to get laid or at least blow his load. There wasn't any chance for it deployed.

"Get her to suck you off," I told him. "She won't get pregnant from that."

There. Problem solved.

"Think we'll ever fit back in here?" Buck wondered, glancing around, Kenzie forgotten. The only thing visible in the dark was the backside of the house and a hint of Gramps' workshop beyond.

"Who the hell knows. I didn't survive drown-proofing to plant wheat and drive a fucking tractor for a living."

"Do you miss it?" Buck cocked his head with the usual tilt.

The back stoop light cast a glow across his face. His blond hair was cut military short. He hadn't shaved in a few days, but he still couldn't grow a damn beard. Not even a mustache. An inch taller than me, Buck was leaner. He was a faster swimmer, but I had him in hand-to-hand combat. Not that anyone from around here understood anything about what our lives entailed. What we endured, so they could fuck beside a bonfire.

"Sparks?" I ran my hand over the back of my neck. It was late August and summer was still hanging on. Barely. The air was cool, and this was Montana. We had another week to go before we were due back in San Diego, but the chance for the weather to turn was always a possibility this far north and at this higher altitude. "I miss snow."

Buck sighed. "I don't think I can ever go on a beach vacation. Shit, I hate sand."

I had to laugh. Afghanistan was hot as hell and a fucking sandbox. That shit got everywhere. In places I never thought possible.

"I got this," I told him. "I can carry the keg by myself. Go have fun with Kenzie." I had no intention of cock blocking my best friend. We were on fucking leave. Our commanding officers expected us to unwind and fuck.

"What about you?" he asked.

I lifted the keg from the tub, ice sloshing, and sat it in the bed beside me. "What about me?"

"There any pussy around here you want to tap?"

Yeah, there definitely was. Indigo. Buck's sister. His smart, gorgeous, barely eighteen sister. The one who'd followed us around when she'd been a kid. Who'd done shit all to get her big brother's attention.

When we left for boot camp, she'd been thirteen. But now?

Holy fuck. Indi wasn't a little kid any longer. She was a beauty. Blonde hair down her back that she no longer wore in two braids. A toned, curvy body with full, high tits. An ass that could probably crack walnuts. Smart and funny and familiar in that coming-home sort of way. How did I know all this?

The Buchanans had had me over for dinner a few nights ago, and there she was. All tanned skin. Full lips. Bold blue eyes that tracked my every move.

I'd gotten one look at her, and my dick had gone instantly hard.

For Buck's little sister.

He'd seen the way I'd stared. Maybe a second too long because he gave me a look. An *I'm going to cut your dick off and feed it to you before you even know what happened* glare.

I'd never dealt with the bro code before because, hell, I didn't lust after jailbait. But Indi wasn't little or a girl any longer. She was perfect.

Perfectly off-limits.

So I answered my best friend the only way I could so as not to lose my dick. "Nah."

He tipped his head toward the house. "You sure?"

I glanced that way and saw a lacy white bra dangling from the screen door handle.

He grinned. "I don't need to speak five languages to understand that's for you."

I hopped down from the bed, my boots hitting the dirt of the driveway. I pulled the keg onto the tailgate, then slid it toward him.

"Here. I'll go see what's going on inside."

I was fine with one-night stands. In fact, that was the only kind of sex I had. It wasn't like a SEAL led the nine-to-five lifestyle. Girlfriends and wives didn't know when their men would come walking through the door. Or if they would ever again.

I knew the chances of survival being in the military, especially being a SEAL. I took it on voluntarily. Even my grandparents understood the risks since Gramps had been in Vietnam. But I wasn't putting a woman through that fuckery. It wasn't fair to her.

The bra on the screen door? Whoever it belonged to was in my house. Uninvited. Even if she was—very obviously—requesting sex. I didn't like being surprised. Ambushed, even with pussy. Because I'd been trained to stay alive. To watch out for shit like this.

But this wasn't war, and the woman not wearing a bra? She sure as hell wasn't my enemy. Since my dick was also on vacation, it got hard at what was being offered.

Buck slapped me on the back. "Have fun."

He hoisted the dripping keg up onto his shoulder and hoofed it back toward the bonfire. He disappeared into the darkness, and I went to snag the bra off the door. Based on the size of the cups, the woman who'd discarded it had a nice handful. Perfect.

I went into the familiar kitchen. The house was quiet, only the light over the stove was on. After peeking into the family room and finding it empty, I went up the back steps to my bedroom. A sliver of light seeped out from beneath the closed door. I took a second to adjust my now-hard dick before turning the doorknob.

Holy fucking hell.

It was Indi, and she was naked.

In my bed.

"Hey, Ford."

CHAPTER ONE

Nine Years Later

INDIGO

THE HEEL of my hiking boot skidded ten feet down the slick embankment before I managed to stop. At least I stayed on my feet—*oof.* I slipped a second time and slid another six feet on my ass, which was now muddy and soaked.

Great. Just perfect.

I lurched back to standing. A bolt of lightning followed instantly by a crack of thunder meant being exposed. Cold rain pelted my head and shoulders, and every drop registered through my hooded, waterproof jacket. The sudden summer cloudburst turned the already muddy soil of the mountain to the consistency of a soggy bar of soap. The kind that slid out of grasp and had to be chased around the tub while leaving slick remains in its wake.

I needed to find a place to take cover until the storm passed. There were trees taller than me to get hit by lightning, but I wasn't stupid. I needed shelter and now. The trouble was the closest place belonged to Ford Ledger.

God, Ford. The guy I'd been stupid over when I was eighteen. Who'd embarrassed me. No, I'd done a really impressive job of that all on my own. My own tattered pride was the reason I was debating whether to step foot on his land, even in a flash storm.

Yeah, it had been that bad. He was the extremely hot but jerky best friend of my brother, David. Or better known by his friends as Buck. Ford was the last guy on Earth I wanted to ask for or accept help from. His grandmother might be there. She'd let me in with open arms and dry clothes, but I couldn't risk it. Not if it meant seeing or dealing with Ford. So there was no chance in hell I'd show up at his door.

Not even if the mountain turned into a volcano and erupted.

Sparks was a small town, but somehow I'd managed to avoid Ford in the months since he retired from combat to do God-knows-what on his land. That was because I would've rather frozen to death than have a one-on-one conversation with him. I didn't need to be told off and turned away. Again.

Yeesh—ack!

I slid again. I was completely off-trail now, and getting back to the path and following it probably wasn't my best bet. It was a ninety-minute hike without any cover to the trailhead where I parked. Not even a rocky outcropping to shelter beneath.

I looked down the mountainside toward Ford's property through the pouring rain. It was hard to see, but there was an old greenhouse, one I never remembered. Although the one time I'd been to his house, I'd been more interested in his bedroom than anywhere else on the huge property. I could hole up in the greenhouse until the storm passed. I wasn't the first Montanan to seek refuge from a neighbor.

I hunched my shoulders against the wind and rain and changed the angle of my descent, picking my footholds carefully to avoid more sliding and slipping. A lot of good it did me. I spilled three more times before I reached the property line. The barbed wire on the low fence looked new and aggressive like it was built for more than just keeping stray cattle in or out. Going to the nearest post, I braced on it as I climbed the strands of taut wire. Even taking great care, I ripped my pants climbing over it.

"Fuck," I muttered, wiping rain off my nose and setting off again.

I made it to the greenhouse—which was also in better repair than I expected—and tested the door. It was locked.

"Seriously?" I said to no one.

Who locked a greenhouse? I might hate the guy, but I'd known Ford my whole life. Sure, the only time I'd seen him since that fateful, naked night years ago was at Buck's memorial. Pot was legal to grow now, but I couldn't imagine Ford or his grandmother cultivating plants that had to be kept safe from theft. What was the guy up to? A lock only meant one thing. He was shady. Like Buck, whose last actions as a SEAL were supposedly less than heroic. Hell, they said he'd *murdered* someone.

I pushed that thought away like usual because I didn't want to think about the shit that we were told about my brother. The things he couldn't answer. Because he was dead.

Dropping my backpack on the ground, I grabbed the multipurpose tool I always carried. I tried to jimmy the lock, but after several frustrating attempts, I gave up. Finding a rock, I smashed a low window and used it to clear the remaining shards. Grabbing my bag and shoving it through the opening, I then hoisted myself through next and tumbled inside.

Christ, I was wet.

I left a puddle which only grew larger as I shook like a Golden Retriever to get the water off my jacket. My hiking pants were soaked through, despite being made of water-wicking material. They were no competition against this rainstorm. My boots, well, they were at least five pounds heavier than normal and caked with mud.

I was a mountain guide, used to things like this, but it didn't make being soggy and cold any more pleasant. Thankfully, I didn't have to paste on a smile for paying tourists. Tell them that a little rain made a vacation more memorable. I glanced around. "What the hell?" I whispered to myself.

There weren't any plants. The space had been converted into a gym. A gym like at a fancy hotel.

Two treadmills and a rowing machine were at one end. Racks held free weights, and in the corner were neatly placed kettlebells. The floor wasn't concrete but a grid of cushioning rubber. A giant punching bag hung over the mats on one end.

I glanced up at the glass ceiling, and all I saw was pounding rain. Who knew how long this spring storm would last. I had no intention of putting in a few miles on a treadmill; I had the wilderness outside for that. Except I couldn't sit here in my wet clothes while I waited for the weather to pass. Before the front came in, it had been in the high seventies, and thankfully, the glass kept the space balmy. I sighed, then shivered, even though it was warm.

"Sorry, Ford," I muttered as I toed off the muddy boots. Nah, I wasn't sorry. Getting his fancy home gym muddy wasn't close to what I'd had in mind for getting even after all these years.

I would've been lying, though, if I pretended there wasn't a part of me that didn't want to stick it to him a bit after what he'd done to me. Okay, what I'd done to him, but either way, "the incident" had left a big scar on my confidence—and heart—and created enough shame to pretty much ruin sex for me. It didn't make me any less horny because I'd seen Ford at the grocery store a few months ago. Yeah, I'd hid behind a display of canned peaches, but I'd seen him. He'd changed since the night I offered up my virginity to him on a platter. Back then, he'd been a focused SEAL, all sharp edges and precision. At the funeral, he'd looked older. Weary. The gloss had been gone, but I hadn't paid him all that much attention. But in the pasta aisle? His dark hair had been longer. He had a dang beard like he was settling in well to mountain life, which somehow made me all kinds of aroused.

He still had sharp edges, but they were honed now. As if his focus was laser-sharp.

It made me wonder what all that intensity was like in bed.

Those thoughts were why I was hiding in his greenhouse gym instead of knocking on his front door. I wasn't going to be denied twice. In the same place.

I removed my jacket and stripped off the wet hiking pants. At least my t-shirt and panties were dry. That was about all, though. I hopped on one foot, then the other, to take off my wet socks. They weren't going to be fun to put back on, but I'd worry about that later.

The pounding of the rain on the plastic roof must've drowned out all other sounds because I had no idea I was no longer alone until a deep, all-too-painfully familiar voice rumbled behind me.

"Indigo Buchanan."

I jumped a foot and screamed then spun around.

There, standing in jeans and a soggy black shirt was an older, broader, bigger Ford Ledger. And he was holding a gun. He ran a hand over his mountain man beard as he raked his gaze over every inch of me.

"You have a real habit of taking your clothes off and making yourself at home where you don't belong."

CHAPTER
TWO

FORD

I PUT the safety back on the M9 I'd palmed when the security system alerted us that someone had breached the fence at the property line and tucked the weapon in the waistband of my pants. This time when the sensor went off, it hadn't been a deer jumping the fence. Or a bear.

No, it was Indigo "Indi" Buchanan.

I debated if I'd rather wrestle a bear than this woman. Fuck, no. I wanted to roll around with her. Too much. She'd have claws, and I kind of hoped she bit, just a little. At least that was my dick talking.

I tried—*fuck*, I tried—not to look below her

waist. I couldn't, *shouldn't,* drink in the sight of those long, toned legs. The bare skin that...

No.

Nope.

Fuck—not going to look.

Not going to even think about checking out what color, cut, and style of panties she wore. Not when I remembered all too well what she looked like *out* of them.

In my bed.

Indi.

The woman who haunted my dreams. Who taunted me still, even though this was the first time I'd seen her since she was eighteen—except across the church at Buck's memorial service. All those years ago, Buck and I had been on leave. The summer she'd graduated high school. The night she'd left her bra dangling as an invitation and climbed naked in my bed with the intention of letting me punch her V card. The night Buck had found us thirty seconds after I'd covered my eyes and told her to get out. He'd wanted to hand me my balls for breakfast.

Now? She wasn't for me even though she was no longer jailbait. She never had been, and she never would be, no matter how fucking gorgeous she was.

She was my *dead* best friend's little fucking sister. Off-limits.

I'd promised Buck I hadn't and wouldn't touch her. It had been because of the bro code before that night, then after, Buck explicitly told me to stay the fuck away from her. No screwing around with younger sisters.

Even if they weren't young or little any longer. Hell, she was... I did the math...twenty-seven and standing half-naked and dripping wet in the old greenhouse we'd converted into a gym.

Indi's eyes flashed, teeth clenched tight. Besides wet, her skin appeared wind-chapped, but there was no mistaking the additional flush crawling down her neck.

Clenching my fists, I avoided reaching out and wiping away the rain dripping down her cheeks. Back then and even now, one touch, and I knew I'd be fucking ruined. Because her skin would be silky soft against my calloused palms. Sweet beneath my lips. She was spirited and wild, and I knew her passion would have no depths. I'd drown in her.

I *would not* break a promise to the man who'd bled out in my arms. The man whose death—and actions leading up to it—I was investigating and intended to solve, even if it catapulted me to my own early grave.

It was clear she wasn't here bent on seduction. Sure, seeing her like this was sexy as hell, but there was no peekaboo lace or sultry looks. No lacy bras in my grasp. She looked like a dunked cat. A gorgeous, perfect dripping cat.

Fuck, now I thought about her pussy. How it might be dripping. I growled.

"Ford Ledger. Still an ass, I see," she shot back, tipping up her chin and glaring.

I deserved it, and not just for my unnecessary taunt. If I'd had any honor left at all, I'd have gone to the Buchanan house in town or even their hardware store every week to see what I could do to help Buck's parents. To try to ease their pain and grief over their dead son. But they hadn't wanted to see me—*too painful*, his mother had said at the funeral —and I couldn't face them again, either. What could I say besides their son's death was my fault. Buck had gotten into something and hadn't confided in me. Hell, he'd been accused of buying drugs and murdering Abdul Tareen, a local Afghan law enforcement officer looking into the case a few weeks before his death. It wasn't fucking possible. I knew Buck, and he wouldn't do that.

Still, he'd been involved in something. And I had been his Master Chief and should've known what the fuck had been going on with him. Protected him from the shit he'd gotten into—whatever it was.

No, I couldn't face any of the Buchanans until I figured out who killed Buck and why. The day he'd died, he'd left the US base without authorization. Yes, he'd gone to meet someone in the village—I didn't know who. Knowing Buck, there had been a damn good reason. One that got him killed. I intended to figure out who was behind it all.

I took a few steps forward. Not because I wanted to be closer to Indi. Hell, no.

Because I wanted a better look at her face while I questioned her. Not that she required interrogating. She wasn't on some kind of mission to destroy me. No, it was pretty obvious what happened here.

"Got caught in the storm?" I asked. I was soaked too just from the sprint from the house, but my clothes were staying the fuck on.

She shoved her wet honey-colored hair out of her face and cocked a hip like she was ready to stand her ground with me. In just a shirt.

Which was cute. Damn cute. I was a fucking SEAL. *Former* fucking SEAL. I did shit for exercise that would kill a regular guy. And she was a tiny slip of a woman in comparison. If she kicked my shin, I wouldn't even feel it. Although the way she was looking at me, I expected her to aim a little higher.

"Sure did." She said it like a challenge, lifting her chin at a haughty angle. That cockiness had my dick going rock hard.

I was still having a helluva time not looking down at those legs. Especially with the way she stuck one out at an angle toward me.

"So you decided to break into my greenhouse."

She shrugged as she glanced around, taking in all the exercise equipment. "Shelter's shelter," she explained as if I didn't know a thing or two about survival skills.

I cocked an eyebrow and crossed my arms over my chest. My t-shirt was damp against my forearms. "Rather than try the house?"

She rolled her eyes like a brat. "Can you blame me? You're not exactly the welcome wagon."

Now I was offended. "You think I'd turn Buck's little sister away in a storm?" I asked incredulously.

She flinched at the mention of her brother—and probably the fact that I'd done just that once before —and I immediately regretted it, but then I was distracted by something else.

Her tits.

They were covered—completely covered—but her nipples still poked through the thin material. They were stiff and erect under her Sparks Outdoor Adventure company t-shirt. Even after all this time, I remembered how pink those tips were, how they were upturned and... fuck, lickable. Even though I hadn't gotten close enough to do any licking.

They were like that now, probably from the cold. Or the rain. Except, wouldn't I have noticed them right away? No, it seemed like they'd gotten stiff talking to me, which, unfortunately, made me harder.

Buck's sister, I reminded myself. She was Buck's sister. Fuck.

"Jesus, I'm not just Buck's little sister." She raised her hands and made air quotes to go along with the sass. "I'm my own woman, Ford. I was then. I am now. How did you even know I was in here?" She turned the convo back to me.

I'd been out of the military and back in Montana for less than a year. One of the first things I'd done to the place when I returned was to set up top-notch security. I didn't fucking trust anyone. Especially not the US government who was supposed to have my back. The only people I trusted were my grandparents—and Gramps had been gone for two years now —and my team.

I'd called in Kennedy, Alpha Team 5 expert data analyst, who'd left the service right after I had. After the shit that went down, he'd chosen not to reup. Instead, he'd showed up in a fucking snowstorm and gotten to work, putting up sensors to let us know of anything over four feet tall—keeping the alarms from pinging with every wild animal—crossed onto the land or was moving about. Every inch of the Ledger land was monitored. The compound the men and I were building was like a fortress with impenetrable, invisible walls.

Gram had welcomed me back with open arms, regardless of the military's reason for kicking me out. She'd also welcomed Kennedy, Hayes and Taft. Said it had been boring around here and was having fun watching us set up my new venture: Alpha Mountain Security.

"I knew the second you stepped over my fence," I said.

She tossed her hands up and shook her head. "You know what? This isn't worth it. If you're going to be an asshole about me getting out of the weather and wave your freaking gun around then—"

"Why were you out in it in the first place?" I

hadn't been *waving* a gun. Jesus. Either way, I wasn't going to correct her about that. She didn't know about my post-SEAL mercenary work. How I took jobs needing my military-trained skill sets that paid a shit-ton more than a Master Chief.

If she thought I was an asshole mountain man, all the better.

"It wasn't raining when I headed out, you idiot," she snapped.

"You should be better prepared."

Her mouth fell open, and I had a feeling if smoke could come out of her ears, it would be now. "Prepared? I had everything I needed, and I found shelter, more than others out hiking today probably did."

"No one else ended up here." I raised my hand indicating not just the greenhouse but my property.

"You sure? Maybe I'm to pull your attention one way while my team of tourist hikers overrun your house."

That sass. Holy shit, she needed her ass spanked for that sass.

"And part of that plan was to take off your pants? I didn't think you teased people that way... any longer."

The second I said that, I knew it had been a mistake. A low blow. A true asshole move. I bit my tongue, but I couldn't take it back. While I'd been pissed she'd been in my bed and offered herself all those years ago, I always appreciated that she recognized her sexual needs, even at eighteen. She hadn't been shy about them. No, she'd fucking owned her sexuality, and I'd snubbed it. And her.

The biggest thing I'd thought of since then? She'd come to me. To my bed. Offered that gorgeous pussy and sweet cherry to me. *Me.*

Now? Fuck... I was a dick.

She flushed then glared daggers. "I'd rather be out in the storm than do this with you." She tried to breeze past me, but I caught her elbow.

What a mistake. Total. Fucking. Mistake. Now I knew how soft and smooth her skin was. Caught her rain and cucumber scent. She was close enough that I wanted to touch other parts of her, too. Lift her up, so she'd wrap those bare legs around my waist, press her against the glass and have my way with her. Lay her over the weight bench and push those thighs nice and wide. Have her bend over the weight rack and take her from behind. Get deep inside that sweet pussy I'd craved for years.

Yeah, thoughts of her forbidden body had gotten me through some of the worst fucking hellholes.

"Stop." I sounded gruff like I was dressing down

a team member, not protecting a friend's sister. Even if it was from only a storm.

I would've dialed it back, but that would have been a mistake, too. I couldn't encourage any feelings on her part—not that she even remotely still harbored the same ones she'd had at eighteen. She thought I was an asshole, and that would keep her away.

Because if I found her in my bed again, I wasn't sure if I'd turn her away. I'd take her. Intimately. *Aggressively.*

I wasn't a gentle lover.

"You're not going anywhere but into the house where you can warm up and dry your clothes."

"Oh *really?*" she fumed. "You have a lot of nerve, Ford. You haven't said ten words to me or my parents since Buck's death, and now you're acting like we're all still buddy-buddy? You didn't want me all those years ago, and you think I'm back for what... more? More humiliation and embarrassment? I don't think so." She yanked her arm out of my grasp and tried to pass me again.

I could've stopped her. Easily. Could've wrapped an arm around her waist to keep her from the door, or tossed her over my shoulder and carried her to the house. Hell, I could've even apologized, but the list was so long, I didn't know where to even start.

She could stay here and wait out the storm, but there was no way I was letting her do that. There was a much easier way to get her to do what I wanted, and it had me smirking. I might fight against having Indi beneath me, but she sure as hell was going to do what I said.

I grabbed her wet clothes and backpack from the ground then beat her to the door. "See you in the house," I tossed out before walking out into the storm, letting the rain cool my need for the one woman I could never have.

"Ford!" she yelled. "You fucking asshole. I'm going to—"

The pounding rain cut off the rest of her words as I made my way across the field to the house. I was smiling for the first time in months.

CHAPTER
THREE

INDIGO

FORD TOOK MY PANTS. He took my fucking pants!

I stared out the open door and into the rain.

"That *asshole*," I swore.

I technically could have stayed in the greenhouse until the weather let up then hiked back to my truck bare-legged and panty-assed, but I wasn't dumb. Ford knew that. The fucker.

I had no choice but to tuck my feet into my soggy hiking boots—which he'd so *generously* left—and trudged through the rain to the house. In just my t-shirt. Ford's property was huge, and it took a few minutes to cut across it. I took the time to mutter and swear like *I'd* been the one in the Navy. By the time I stomped through the back screen door, I was fuming and soaked.

"Listen, you asshole, I—"

A man held up his hands at my verbal attack, but it wasn't Ford.

I stopped short and shut my mouth.

Oh God. *Another* guy saw me in my panties today. It kept getting worse.

He was built like a lumberjack and was hot as hell. Jesus, what was in the water over here? I pegged him at six-four and well over two hundred pounds. All muscle. The guy had zero body fat, and I could tell because his t-shirt was practically painted on his sculpted torso. Strangely, he had a lollipop tucked in the pocket of his cheek.

I wasn't the only one doing a body scan. His blue eyes roved over every inch of me. Every wet, bare or drenched inch of me.

"I'm not the asshole, sweetheart." His voice was deep and rough. "Trust me, I have more pleasurable ways of getting a woman wet." He winked.

Holy shit, who was this guy?

I glanced away from that megawatt smile when heavy footfall came down the back stairwell. The one I'd once used to sneak up into Ford's bedroom that fateful night when he and my brother had been on leave. There'd been a party. I'd been invited, and I'd naively thought that meant he was interested.

His grandparents had been out of town, I guessed, since they hadn't been home when I'd snuck in. I didn't remember. All that stuck was the unpleasant shock on Ford's face when he'd found me in his bed and the sound of his curse echoing in my ears before he told me to cover myself and get out.

Ugh.

Ford paused on the last step in only a pair of jeans, top button undone. His shirt was missing and a towel was draped over his broad, bare shoulders.

A dog came down the steps behind him and trotted over to me, tail wagging. He was square and brown and looked up at me with eyes that said he was now my new best friend.

I patted his head and scratched behind his ear. "Who's this?"

"That womanizer is Roscoe," the other guy said.

I smiled down at him as he leaned his weight against my leg. "Such a good boy," I praised, and I swore he grinned at me.

"That dog has zero shame," Ford muttered.

That had me looking up from Roscoe.

Holy shit. I'd never seen a man built like him... except maybe the other guy in the room, but my ovaries only perked up at the sight of Ford.

With his hair longer and a beard, Ford looked so different than the man I once knew. He'd been so precise. So focused. He wouldn't have dared let even a hair on his head be unruly. But now? He was far from having the Grizzly Adams appearance, but he looked like a mountain man. My clit pulsed at the sight of him, making me want to jump him and throttle him in equal measure. The washboard abs and the dark happy trail didn't hurt either.

"Roscoe's one thing, but you leave her the fuck alone," Ford growled at the guy. When his gaze turned my way, his jaw clenched. "Fuck, woman."

He grabbed the slung towel and moved to hold it out in front of me. For a second, I thought he was repulsed by what he saw, but I glanced down and noticed my t-shirt was sodden and clung to me like a second skin. Even with a utilitarian sports bra and panties, nothing was hidden. I could see the little bumps around my nipples and...oh God, was that camel toe?

I snagged the towel and held it in front of me.

Ford spun on his bare foot and pointed at the

guy although the only reason I knew that was because his right arm was out. Ford was too big for me to see around, and that seemed to be his point because he said, "That's Buck's little sister you're eye-fucking."

All I could do was stare at Ford's defined delts and lats. From his wide shoulders, those back muscles tapered in a solid V to a trim waist. Why did I have to hate someone so perfect? My body didn't care that he was an asshole.

"I'm sure the woman knows she's hot."

I bit my lip when I heard Ford's growl. Roscoe nudged me with his nose since I'd stopped petting him, but I was distracted by the men's argument.

"Why is she without pants?"

"She took them off."

"Why?"

"They were wet."

"So's the rest of her."

"She was out in the storm, dumbass."

"Without pants?"

"I have them."

"Why the fuck do *you* have her pants?"

Their conversation went back and forth, and I tried to step around Ford, but he threw his arm out as if stopping short in a car.

I ducked and went under it.

"I'm right here," I muttered. "I have a name. And usually pants. I'm Indi."

"Buck's sister," not-Ford said.

"That's right. Indigo Buchanan." I stuck my hand out for the guy.

"Kennedy." He took a step toward me and held out his big paw, but Ford moved and swatted it away.

"You were part of Buck's team, too." I remembered some of what Buck had told me and my parents about his team through video calls and emails.

Kennedy nodded and gave me a small smile that crinkled the corner of his eyes. Then the smile disappeared, and he took the lollipop out of his mouth. "Real sorry about Buck. None of us will ever recover from the loss."

I swallowed hard. I couldn't say anything, so I only nodded. Not wanting to think about how much I missed my brother or the fact that he turned out to be a murderer, I switched topics.

"Kennedy. Right." I cleared my throat. "I remember Buck mentioning you guys are all named after presidents."

Kennedy grinned again. His teeth were extra bright with his California surfer tan and looks although his reddish hair wasn't overly long or wild.

"That's right." He cocked his head toward Ford. "Our leader here, along with Buck, started it off."

"Ford and Buchanan, you mean," I replied, referencing the coincidence the two friends both had presidential names. He nodded. "Your real name is Kennedy?"

He winked again. "Nah. Your man here gave it to me."

"Why Kennedy?" I asked.

He put the lollipop back in his mouth and crunched down. "Because the ladies like me."

I had to laugh at that. From what I could tell, that was probably the case. Compared to Ford, he was laid back. Easy going. Charming.

"I've got you out of your pants, haven't I?" he asked.

"Okay, that's enough, Romeo." Ford moved to stand in front of me again. Out of the corner of my eye, I saw Roscoe settle onto a dog bed in the corner.

I whipped around and poked Ford in his bare chest. His bare, hard, warm chest. I took a second to process that, then got on with my anger. "Listen up, asshole."

"Fuck, woman." Ford tugged the towel out of my

free hand and wrapped it around my waist, grabbing the two ends and holding them in front of me. When I turned, I'd given Kennedy my backside.

"You're the one who stole my pants. If you've got a problem with my bare ass, then maybe you shouldn't have done that."

"I don't have a problem with your bare ass, but I have a problem with Kennedy seeing it."

"My bare ass is not your responsibility."

His dark eyes narrowed, and his jaw clenched so hard I wasn't sure how his back teeth didn't crack.

"Can we stop saying *bare ass*? Also, every inch of you is my responsibility."

I glared. He glared. He had no reason—or right—to be protective.

"Since when? If I remember correctly, you didn't want anything to do with my bare ass or any other *inch* of me."

"Your eighteen-year-old, barely legal ass that was in my bed?"

My cheeks flamed and shame swamped me.

I grabbed the towel and kept it wrapped around my waist. "Give me my pants, and I'll put them on just as fast as I did that night. I wouldn't want Mrs. L–your grandmother–to see me like this."

"It's okay for Kennedy, though?" he countered.

"I didn't know Kennedy was even here."

"I have three other men living here now. And Gram's off on some senior group field trip."

Four men on the property?

Kennedy came over and stood beside us. "All right, you two." His hand went between our bodies like a ref at a boxing match. "Sweetheart, it's raining something fierce out there, as you well know. Let's get your clothes dry, and I'll drive you back to town."

"Thank you."

"I'll grab one of my shirts, and you can wear that in the meantime."

"No fucking way is she wearing one of your shirts," Ford countered.

Kennedy only smiled.

"You want her to wear a towel or blanket until her clothes dry?"

I liked Kennedy more and more by the minute.

"She's not wearing your shirt," Ford snapped.

Kennedy sighed as if trying to have a conversation with a stubborn preschooler. "Fine. Top of the stairs is the linen closet, sweetheart. There are some flannel sheets and you can grab one. Bathroom's across the hall. Bring your wet things down, and they'll go in the dryer."

I nodded. The faster my clothes dried, the faster I could be out of here.

I took the steps to the second floor but paused at the top when I heard their voices.

"*Sweetheart?* What the fuck? She's Buck's little sister!" Ford snapped.

"She's not little. She's all woman. Every inch. Believe me, I saw."

I thought I heard Ford growl again, but it didn't carry well up the steps.

"You're not touching her."

"Why? Are you going to tap that?"

Tap that. I was now a *that*.

"Nobody is going to tap that."

Nobody? Excuse me? My sex life was none of Ford's business. He certainly didn't have a say in whether I slept with Kennedy or the two other mystery men staying here or anyone else. He missed his chance at being a part of that, and he sure as hell wasn't going to take over the controlling big brother act now that Buck was gone.

"Why the hell not?"

"She's Buck's sister."

"You've said that five fucking times. She's what, mid-twenties? A grown-ass woman who can speak for herself. Besides, I'm sure some other guy claimed that sweet prize since you didn't."

They really were a bunch of foul-mouthed sailors. I wasn't thrilled about my virginity being a topic of their guy talk. I had planned to give it to Ford that night, but instead, gave it to a guy in my dorm a few months later, in the first semester of college. If Ford hadn't wanted it, then I hadn't cared who took it, only that it was gone.

"Fuck, Kennedy. What the hell is wrong with you?"

"Me? You stole her fucking pants."

I didn't stick around for more. Tiptoeing, I found the linen closet and the soft sheets Kennedy mentioned. While Ford was military precise, I had a feeling it was his grandmother, Mrs. L, who'd made the linens so organized.

I needed out of this house. Ford brought back memories I didn't want to resurface. Same went for the room just down the hall. Not only because he'd been so close to Buck, had been there when he'd died, but because of how I'd loved him—or imagined I had. I knew now it was a schoolgirl crush. I'd been naive and stupid.

I wasn't either any longer.

I stepped into the bathroom initially to just

shuck the wet t-shirt. Once I had it off though, the shower seemed to be calling to me. I removed my sports bra and panties, hung the wet clothes on a towel rack, and turned the water to hot. I stepped in and quickly rinsed the mud from my skin.

Not wanting to linger because, this time around, I didn't relish being caught naked in Ford's house– again–I finished up and used one of the towels I found stacked on a shelf to dry off. I'd probably have to take another shower at home with a ton of condi-tioner to untangle my bedraggled hair, but at least I was clean. I wrapped the sheet around my body and marched back down the stairs with my damp clothes. Ford was there waiting for me, but Kennedy had disappeared. So had Roscoe.

Ford took my things—with his eyes focused anywhere in the room but at me—and stalked away to the laundry room. When he returned, he took a mug out of the cabinet. "You want something warm to drink? We have coffee. No tea. Hot chocolate because Kennedy has a sweet tooth." He raised an unruly dark brow. "So do you, if I recall."

I ignored the liquid warmth that spilled into my gut at the fact that he remembered anything about me at all, other than the bedroom incident I wanted to permanently delete from both our minds.

"It's a summer storm, not a blizzard."

I had this inane need to prove to him that I was no longer the kid sister. He may be a former Navy SEAL, but I was damn capable myself. I led all kinds of wilderness trips during the summer and took outdoor adventurers on cross-country ski trips in the winter. In fact, during the busy season, I was in the backcountry more than I was at home. This rainstorm had caught me on a solo, for-fun hike on one of my days off.

He stepped closer, close enough that I had to tip my head up to glare back at him. "Well, you still look cold." He brushed one finger over the goosebumps on my arm. His touch made every inch of skin on my body tingle. Every nerve-ending fire.

My lips parted, and I suddenly found breathing impossible.

"Come on, Indi. We don't need to have a stand-off on whether you drink hot cocoa in my kitchen or not." He still sounded gruff, but his tone was softer than before. Probably in the range of conciliatory for him. "Truce?"

Truce? Could I let what happened all those years ago just... go away? I wasn't the same person I was then. Neither was Ford. He looked nothing like the clean-cut SEAL with that beard. It might be trimmed and neat, but I was sure it didn't match Navy regulations or the man himself.

"Fine. Hot chocolate..." I swallowed down the unsettled emotions Ford brought out in me. "...sounds good."

Still, I stepped back. A truce didn't mean I wanted him touching me because I'd felt way too much with that one simple caress. Stupid, traitorous body.

He narrowed his eyes like this was an important point. "With milk or water?"

I couldn't stop the laugh that tumbled from my lips. "Milk. I need all the calories I can get after today's hike."

He turned and pulled a gallon jug of whole milk from the fridge and poured it into the mug. "What were you doing out there alone?" He glanced at me over his shoulder as he popped open the microwave and placed the mug inside then turned it on.

I shrugged. "I prefer hiking alone."

His brows popped at that. "Yeah?" He leaned back against the counter and folded his arms over his chest. He'd put a t-shirt on while I'd been in the shower, but the thin fabric didn't hide how strong he was. How fit. He might've been out of the Navy, but there was no question he kept up with PT. He looked more lumberjack than sailor. Maybe he chopped wood for exercise. There certainly wasn't any ocean to swim in.

"It's better than entertaining a group of hikers for hours on end," I explained then adjusted the sheet.

"With the outdoor adventure company in town."

I shouldn't have been pleased that he was aware of what I did. Sparks was a small town. Everyone knew everything about each other. But he and I hadn't had a single interaction since he returned. As far as I knew, he'd been holed up here on his property like a wild mountain man. His grandfather had died a few years ago, so he lived here with his grandmother. And now, I learned with three other men.

Which seemed...odd. I hadn't stopped to wonder what Ford was doing up here. Apparently, more than just living off his pension or the land. Especially if he had some kind of sensor or something that picked up I'd crossed his fence line. And the lock on the greenhouse. Who needed to lock up gym equipment five miles outside of a tiny Montana town?

"Yeah. Don't get me wrong—I'm grateful I can make a living doing what I love. But I don't need a buddy on my days off."

The microwave beeped, and Ford pulled the mug

of hot milk out and emptied a packet of chocolate powder into it, stirring briskly with a spoon.

"I don't like the idea of you out there on your own."

I bristled. "I can take care of myself. I take sole responsibility for entire groups of hikers in the backcountry."

"Don't you have a partner with Sparks Outdoor Adventures?"

At the mention of Brandon, I grimaced. But color me surprised that Ford knew this much about my business. I ran that place more than Brandon did—everyone in town probably knew that. My name was even more synonymous with Sparks Outdoor Adventure than Brandon's.

"He's my boss, not a partner," I said quickly. I was no longer sleeping with Brandon. *That* had been a short-term mistake.

Huge mistake.

I learned a very important rule: Never screw your boss, no matter how friendly, laid-back and easygoing he made everything seem. When things went south, work got really awkward. Even if I barely saw him at work. Brandon was having a perpetual temper tantrum since I told him I couldn't handle a relationship. Right now or ever. I'd given him the old

It's not you, it's me line. That I was still grieving Buck's death and just couldn't think about a relationship.

I just couldn't think about a relationship *with him.* For so many reasons. He was a slacker for one. And since he couldn't find my clit with a topo map and a compass, he'd left me unsatisfied.

Now he was talking about moving out of Sparks. Which meant I needed to figure out how to scrape together enough money to make him an offer on the business, or I'd lose my job. Sparks wasn't plentiful in them, and I sure as hell wasn't the type to work behind a desk all day.

"Oh, you seem more like a business partner. I heard you run everything over there." Ford narrowed his gaze and studied me. "Wait—were you two—"

"It's none of your business," I snapped, refusing to meet his eyes.

"I see." He handed me the mug of hot chocolate, and the damn sheet slipped when I reached for it, giving Ford a flash of nip.

"Jesus," he bit out, eyes darkening. He turned abruptly away. "I'll get you one of my shirts."

I couldn't keep from smirking as he stalked out of the kitchen. Did my bare breast just fluster the unflappable tough guy, Ford Ledger? The guy I lusted after for all of my teen years? The one who I equally craved and despised?

Could it be... Ford *did* find me attractive? All these years, I'd thought he'd been repulsed when I'd offered myself up that long-ago night. He'd cursed and covered his eyes and snarled at me to get out of his bed. Of course, it hadn't helped that Buck had been right behind him and had seen everything. Literally, all of me, which was gross.

Buck—the asshole—had hauled me out to my car telling me I'd acted like a slut. The next day, he'd given me some stupid sexist lecture on how guys didn't respect girls who threw themselves at men. Even though I'd tried to shake it off, the scars both of them left on me still festered to this day.

But what if Ford hadn't been repulsed? What if he'd been... tempted?

Maybe it had been my brother's presence that made it awful and weird. Maybe it hadn't been all me. Then why was he still being an asshole? A truce was one thing, but he'd taken my clothes. Sure, I was stubborn, but still. He was grumpy and intense and moody. And hot.

I took a sip of the hot cocoa and moaned softly. It totally hit the spot. Ford was right, I was still cold—I hadn't stayed in the hot shower long enough to really warm up, and my hair was still wet.

He returned with a Navy—the organization, not the color—t-shirt and a pair of boxers.

"Thanks."

I set the mug down, and he reached out.

I slapped his hand away, surprised.

He wasn't reaching for my boob, but my pendant about my neck.

He held it in his fingers, eyed it for a time.

"I was with Buck when he got this for you," he said, his voice low. He studied it as if remembering the event. It was gold with decorative filigree and a blue center stone on a simple chain. I glanced from it to Ford. He was so close, I had to tip my head back. His eyes were so blue but cold. The beard had flecks of red and a thin scar sliced through the tan on his forehead.

He smelled of man and sunshine and some kind of soap. Like pine and leather.

"I... I never take it off," I admitted, swallowing hard. "It was the last thing he gave me. The last mail we got from him."

He offered a small nod. "We went to a bazaar in town about three weeks before—"

Before he'd watched him die. Before Buck had

been identified as a murderer, and it was determined that if he'd lived, he'd have been brought up for court-martial. I tugged the sheet up around me as if it could protect me from the hurt of losing Buck and what he'd done. But Ford had been there, beside him when he'd thought of me from thousands of miles away. To fight beside him. To die in his arms.

He let go of the pendant, and I went into the bathroom tucked under the stairs to change. I needed a minute, and so did he. I wiped away tears as I pulled his shirt on. It was huge and so were the boxers, so I rolled the waistband down until it held above my hips. When I returned, Ford sat at the kitchen table next to the place where I'd placed my mug. His gaze raked over me from the top of my head to my bare feet.

The scene looked halfway invitational, so I pulled out the chair beside him and took a seat. If I was hurting from Buck's death, Ford had to as well. He'd *held* Buck as he'd died, and I had to remember he might be big and strong, but he was still a man.

"What are you doing these days, Ford?" I asked, channeling my mother and her skill at small talk.

He toyed with the napkin holder in the center of the table. The furnishings appeared mostly the same as I'd remembered. The sunny yellow wallpaper here in the kitchen. I could see the lace doilies on the armrests on the couch in the living room. He might be in his thirties, but he was living with his grandmother. While she wasn't in the house right now, her presence was everywhere. Here on their land and also in town. She was a well-loved, active woman. I wanted to be like her when I was eighty.

"Security work."

I didn't know what answer I'd expected, but it wasn't that. "What does that mean? Like a bouncer at a bar?"

His ever-present frown deepened. He ran a hand over his beard, and I instantly wondered how it would feel against my inner thighs. "No."

I waited when he didn't elaborate.

"Like special ops for hire," he finally added.

Oh. Whoa. I should've known Ford would still be a bad-ass, even after he left the Navy. It made sense.

"Hence the security-rigged fence and greenhouse. And that's why Kennedy is here with you." I'd been trying to sort that part out, but now it made sense.

He nodded. "The guys and I live in my grandfather's old workshop. We converted it and added on to make it a bunkhouse. Our main base is here, but we travel all over the world for jobs."

"Other guys? You said four of you live here. Are they also from your team?" I didn't know why it made my heart both spin out and speed up to hear about Buck's old team members. To know they were still operating without him. That some had settled here in Sparks. I felt both connected to them and completely left out. I hid my face in the hot cocoa, surprised by the unexpected emotions.

"Yeah. Hayes and Taft are here, too. I'm building a new team. A few others will join when their contracts are up," he said, instead of answering my question. "Business is... brisk."

The kitchen suddenly seemed quiet. It took me a moment to realize why. I glanced out the window to confirm it, past the yellow gingham cafe curtains. I jumped to my feet. "Well, the storm has passed. I'll get out of your hair."

Ford opened his mouth then closed it, scrubbing a hand across his beard again. "Yeah. Okay. I doubt your clothes are dry, though."

"That's okay," I said quickly. I needed to get out of this place. Away from Ford Ledger. Away from the memories. He brought up far too many emotions in me that I'd rather not delve into. "I'll stop by later for them?"

"You're not going out dressed like that," he said,

looking me over. "You're not even wearing underwear."

"I can do whatever I want, Ford." I crossed my arms, suddenly noticing the air on my very bare lady parts. "Remember that."

He sighed and murmured something under his breath, something along the lines of *fuck me.* "I'll drop them by your place. *Of business*," he clarified quickly, making me want to kick him in the nuts for making it so abundantly clear he wasn't interested. Like I hadn't seen that momentary look of hunger when he caught sight of my breast. "I'll drop them by your place of business tomorrow."

Whatever. It didn't matter—I wanted nothing to do with him either.

I'd already grabbed my knapsack from the counter and was shoving my bare feet into my muddy boots by the back door. I hated that he followed me and stood there like he had something he wanted to say.

"Thanks for the hot chocolate," I said in a rush, finishing the second lace. "Let's not do it again soon."

"Bye, Blue."

I stumbled at his use of the childhood nickname he'd given me. His deep rumble echoed after me as I took off at a jog, not caring that I was out hiking in a pair of boxer shorts and Ford's oversized t-shirt or that my car was still a couple of miles away. Or that my panties and bra were in his dryer.

I'd left his place half-dressed before. I'd fled once. It seemed I was doing it again.

CHAPTER FOUR

FORD

I HEFTED my ax and swung down to crack another log. With the sun beating down, I'd ditched my shirt a while ago. Splitting wood was my go-to when I needed to blow off steam, and fuck, in the past three days, I'd prepped firewood for the entire winter. In fact, I had enough to stack in the bed of my truck to take to Buck's parents.

The frustration I was burning through wasn't because I was constantly wracked with guilt over the way I'd handled Buck's death. It also didn't have anything to do with Indi's surprise visit. And I definitely wasn't nursing a set of blue balls after seeing her nearly naked. Again.

Fuck me.

I just had a lot on my mind pulling together my team and figuring out our next moves.

Right.

That's what I told myself, anyway.

Roscoe came over and dropped a stick at my feet. I grabbed the slobber-covered piece of wood and lobbed it across the field. He sprinted after it.

With my back muscles starting to strain, I finished the last log and left the ax embedded in the stump. I'd be back out here soon enough. Using my discarded t-shirt to wipe my brow, I strode across the field to the back door. Roscoe caught up with me, stick in his mouth.

I was still getting used to thinking of the place as mine. I came to live with my grandparents after my dad's death when I was in middle school. He and my mom had been split for years, and my mom had been one of those who'd thought a kid was a burden. I'd felt it hardcore, and our relationship had been shit. My grandparents had wanted me, and hell, I'd wanted them too. Looking back, I'd been desperate for something settled, something safe, and they'd given it to me. I'd come to

Montana and made this mountain my proving ground.

Gramps had died two years ago while I'd been overseas. Fell asleep in his recliner one night and never woke up. Gram had been alone here since then, except for Roscoe, who she said she'd gotten to replace Gramps.

After almost fifteen years in the service, I had never put down roots, never even rented an apartment since I'd been deployed, never needed more than base housing. Hell, I had no real home. Except for here. So when I was rather suddenly dishonorably discharged, I'd tucked tail and come back to be here with Gram. Turned out that it was the perfect spot to start up my new private security firm. Gram had been thrilled to have me back and the idea of having a bunch of my buddies here too. She was far from the typical grandmother. While she baked cookies for all of us, she'd also handed over her sewing room to be used as a temporary command center until the new building was finished.

It was one thing to live on the property to keep an eye on Gram, it was another to sleep in my old bedroom down the hall from her. So now that it was finished, I was in the bunkhouse with Kennedy and the others. For now. The contractors were also working on a cabin for me down by the creek where we'd had all the parties.

I banged the screen door open and stepped in, heading straight for the fridge. Roscoe went to his water dish, dropped the stick in his food bowl, then began to lap up his own drink. The scent of pot roast assaulted me. I glanced at the counter, at the olive green crockpot. Kennedy was just as much a cook as Gram, and he used that slow cooker all the time. I wasn't sure who'd started tonight's dinner, but it made my mouth water.

"Fucker," Kennedy grumbled, catching me drinking milk straight from the jug. "You don't live alone, asshole. If Mrs. L sees you doing that—" He didn't say more, just shook his head.

I kept gulping it down and ignoring him, the cold air from the fridge on my ass.

"So, keeping these as souvenirs?"

I swallowed hard when Kennedy held up Indigo's sports bra and panties, dangling from his fingers.

"Put those down," I snarled before I had the wherewithal to dial back my reaction.

He grinned and set the white scraps swinging. Fuck. I'd just given him more fodder for his damned game.

"Most guys save the lingerie of the women they've already hooked up with not the ones they're pining for." He propped a hip against the counter. He was having way too much fucking fun.

Hayes clomped up the back steps and came into the kitchen, the screen door slapping shut behind his ass. His eyes widened at the dangling bra. "Who the hell got lucky?"

I pulled my Master Chief face—the one that said, *I outrank you, buddy*—and shook my head. "Not another fucking word."

"What's the deal? Are you going to hit that? If not, I am totally—"

I slapped the milk jug on the counter then reached out and snatched Indi's underclothing out of Kennedy's hands. "You're not to go near her." I pointed at him, then at Hayes, but the emphasis was lost with the items in my hands.

"What, are you playing big brother to her now?" Kennedy cocked a brow. I was the serious one, and he was the jokester. The playboy. We'd lived in tight quarters on base and worse on missions, but this kitchen was getting pretty fucking crowded with the three of us in it.

At the mention of Buck, my chest tightened.

"Big brother... now that's a weird kink, but if you get a woman out of a bra like that, it might be a—"

"Fuck off, Hayes," I snapped. "Where the hell is Gram?"

"We dropped her car off with Landers, but she got a text and had plans for coffee. That woman's social calendar makes us look like hermits."

That was true. My grandmother knew everyone in town. Knew all their secrets, too. She was involved in every program from church to the senior program to T-ball fundraiser. She was rarely home, and if she was, she was flitting about with the continuous hopes of firing the weapons we had stored in the bunkhouse.

She could wheedle someone into doing anything, but the four of us had held our ground where my octogenarian grandmother and firearms were concerned.

"So I took her to the Seed n' Feed and dropped her off."

The place was run by Holly Martin. It'd been in her family—like most businesses in Sparks—for generations. What Holly had done, though, was push the envelope of what a seed and feed sold. She'd turned the old grain office into a coffee shop, so now she served more scones than salt licks. When

I worked there when I was sixteen, it'd been a completely different place.

"Said she'd get a ride home later and that she wasn't missing Kennedy's pot roast for anything. Back to the babe with the bra. Was she any good? Does she have sisters?"

I glared.

He held up his hands as if I would kill him with my eyes. Or with my left pinkie, which I could, and he knew it. While Hayes didn't have the same easy charm that Kennedy wore like a second outfit, he was no slouch when it came to women. Dimples creased his darker skin, and his dark brown hair had grown out wavy. He wasn't as tall as Kennedy, but he had a broad chest and could bench press twice his weight.

"I'll get the story eventually," he said.

We were like a bunch of sorority sisters in this place, in each other's business. That was fine and all when he talked about the woman he'd banged at the bar last month, but this was Indi.

Indi. That reminded me I was pissed at Kennedy, so I turned all my anger back his way.

"Buck's last words to me were about taking care of Indi. There's no way in hell I'm letting a douche like you—"

"Buck's last words were about Indi?" Kennedy cut in, frowning. He went to the crockpot, took off the lid, and used a spoon that was on the counter beside it to stir the cubed potatoes. "You never told me that."

"That's Buck's sister's bra?" Hayes asked, his tone now filled with surprise and his hands still up, this time showing he was definitely going to be hands-off now. "Whoa."

I ignored him.

We hadn't been on a mission when he'd died. I'd followed him off base, having his six—or having his back—like a friend and leader should.

Hayes went to the fridge and leaned in to see what was in there.

"Skip the milk," Kennedy advised.

Hayes grabbed the pitcher of sweet tea Gram always had on hand and pulled a glass from the cabinet.

I put my hands on my hips and watched my friend. "Why would I?" I was referring to telling Kennedy what Buck's last words were. "It's hardly relevant."

"What did he say, exactly?" Kennedy was pushing, and it was annoying as fuck. Like probing an open wound with a sharp stick.

I stalked past him to put Indigo's bra and panties back on the neatly folded pile of her clothes on top of the dryer, which was in the laundry room just off the kitchen. The pile I'd said I'd take to her. Yesterday. It was the task I'd been avoiding.

Kennedy—the asshole—put the lid back on the slow cooker and followed me. "What did he say?"

I frowned and ran a hand over my beard. "He told me to look out for Indi," I repeated. For fuck's sake, I didn't need to relive the moment with Kennedy, I saw it almost every night in my nightmares.

Kennedy showed his own flash of irritation. "I asked what he said, exactly."

My gut twisted as I remembered dragging Buck back from the explosion zone. Holding him in my arms as I shouted for help.

I could still feel the heat from the blast. The scents. The screams.

I knelt on the dirty street, carnage all around. Buck was propped on my thighs, destroyed. One leg was gone below the knee. He had a sucking chest wound and blood slid from the corner of his mouth. He was dying, and there was nothing I could do.

His jeep was upside-down behind him, one of the tires on fire, and smoke rose from the engine.

Still, I shouted. "We need help over here!"

It did nothing. Buck was the linguist who knew Arabic. Not me.

I was lost. Helpless. I didn't have my team with me. No comms to get a medic or an evac.

Buck was looking up at me. Staring with those dark eyes. There was no pain in his gaze. He knew he was dying.

Fuck. FUCK! *"Stay with me."*

He shook his head, but the motion was so small. "Indi...safe....watch out."

"What?" I'd demanded. He wasn't making sense.

"Watch out for Indi," he said, his breath shallow and raspy.

I shifted him, tried to press on his chest wound. I'd used my shoelace for a tourniquet above his knee, but it wasn't strong enough. His blood spread across the ground.

"You'll take care of her yourself," I countered. "You got this, Buck."

Five minutes ago, he was whole and fine. I was mentally hating him for making me follow him from base. To figure out what the fuck was up with him lately. Why he was on edge. Distant. Going off solo. Something had been up with him, and it was my job as his best friend and his team leader to help him.

I'd been behind on his shit. And I'd been behind following him. That was why he was ripped up, and I was fine. How I'd missed the blast without a scratch, and he was—

"Indi." His hand flapped up, and he tapped his chest. "They can't know." He coughed and blood dribbled from his lips.

I winced, then held him closer, as if I could put him back together. "She won't know about this," I vowed. "Your parents too. I got you."

But I didn't.

I whipped my head around, trying to figure out what to do. We were almost a mile from base in the middle of the civilian area. This was a local street bazaar now blown to bits. Buck wasn't the only person dying.

I'd been trained to lead, to make split-second decisions. To keep my men alive. I couldn't do anything now. Totally fucking helpless.

"Stay with me, Buck. Stay. Stay..."

I shook off the memory and cleared my throat, as if trying to rid myself of the smoke that was only now in my memory. "It's not important."

Kennedy shrugged but watched me closely. "What if it is? Listen to this—Lincoln called. Someone else is dead from that Ranger team."

After Kennedy set up security on the property

and between jobs for Alpha Mountain, he'd put his expertise to use collecting intel to figure out what the fuck had happened to Buck besides being killed. Two days after his death, word had come down that they'd found evidence he'd murdered an Afghan police officer who was investigating a drug-smuggling operation. One he believed had ties to the U.S. military.

Buck, a murderer. Right.

I'd lost my shit because I knew something was up with my friend since he'd started to take on work with a different division, but shit...drugs? Murder? No chance. I didn't believe it then, and I was even more certain it was a lie now.

Of course, when I started poking into the matter, I was dismissed on bogus charges.

It had been obvious something was up. Someone in the military higher than me or Buck was covering something up.

The men on my former team were too loyal not to side with me. One by one, when their contracts were up, they started to join me to work in private security as we figured out what exactly had happened.

To finance the upgrades to the property—the security, the bunkhouse, the new command center that was almost done, my cabin—we took jobs. Wet work. Security and protection. Rescue.

My former commanding officer, Lincoln, had tossed us a few private security gigs—whether it was out of pity or to keep me from digging into Buck's death more, I couldn't be sure. The upshot was that word of mouth made Alpha Mountain take off. Private mercenary work was lucrative. Lucrative enough to fully fund an entire team of ex-special forces guys, which I would need to continue to grow my business. And if I was going to keep digging into whatever happened back in Afghanistan.

Clients who paid seven figures for a job. We were flush in cash but not answers.

I pushed past Hayes and grabbed the pitcher of tea and shoved it back on the shelf in the fridge. "Who and how?"

Kennedy sent me a meaningful look that had my skin crawling before he even delivered the news. "This is what I've been working on the past few days while you've been moping around over a girl."

I gave him the finger. "Tell me."

"William Gentry. The original translator from the Ranger Beta Team. They're calling it a suicide."

"The original translator? The food poisoning guy?"

Buck had said he'd been asked to fill in for the rangers as a translator because a guy on the team had food poisoning.

"Holy shit. Was it?"

"Too much of a coincidence for me. Two translators from that team dead?"

I stared back at Kennedy as the words sank in. This was news. *Big* news. I didn't want another soldier dead, especially knowing it happened, but this was something. "This means it's not a Buck thing."

"Our buddy couldn't have planned that shit from the grave."

"This proves it's bigger than Buck just as we fucking knew." I slapped Kennedy on the shoulder.

When I glanced Hayes' way, he nodded.

My mind swirled. Buck had been the translator for our team. The Navy quickly learned the fucker had a talent for picking up languages like a hooker did sailors during Fleet Week. After the fill-in for Mr. Food Poisoning, things started to go sideways. Even after the guy recovered, Buck kept getting called in for missions with them. Missions he couldn't discuss with our team. That wasn't anything new, but over the next few weeks and months, he'd grown agitated and withdrawn.

Then he was killed. The bombing was officially ruled as drug-related. They said Buck was parked in front of the building that housed a known drug trafficker. Supposedly, he'd been there to make a transaction. They floated out the theory that the drug dealers had killed him.

Kennedy and I suspected it had been an inside job, especially when a murder rap was added after he was dead and couldn't defend himself.

"So whatever Buck knew—whatever got him killed—this guy knew, too," Kennedy said.

"Sounds like it."

"So back to my question. What exactly did Buck say to you?" he asked.

I shook my head and thought of that moment. "He just said *Indi. They can't know.*"

He scratched his temple. "That's all?"

"Yeah. Like I was going to tell Buck's family about how he died. They have enough with his record. Thank fuck people here in Sparks are forgiving."

Gram was the first to take the Buchanans a casserole and told them how proud she was of Buck. That whatever happened, she knew Buck had done the right thing.

Except I couldn't do that with the Buchanans. Not until I knew the truth. Gram's faith was one thing, but I was the only one stuck with the real nightmare.

"I told you it's not relevant," I added.

Kennedy shrugged and unwrapped a lollipop he pulled from a jar on the counter. "Okay. So he didn't say, keep her safe from Kennedy." His dimples winked as he stuck the candy in his mouth with a grin.

"You're not touching her." I glowered then turned and shared the look with Hayes. "I mean it. I will kill both of you on Buck's behalf."

"Are you filling Buck's shoes protecting her, or is there actually something between the two of you? Because the way you've been chopping wood for days screams of sexual frustration, my friend."

"Yeah, your balls must be so blue, I'm surprised they haven't fallen off yet," Hayes added.

"Fuck off." I picked up Indi's clothes, resolved to finally go into town to the wilderness guide office and drop them off. I wanted to see what kind of outfit she worked for, anyway. It seemed fairly successful, as far as I could tell, but I didn't love that her boss sent her out in the wilderness alone. Or that they'd fucked. Although she was smart and knew how to take care of herself. I may have had a shitty attitude about finding her in my greenhouse, but she'd done all the right things to get out of the dangerous weather.

I'd remember what she looked like standing there in only her t-shirt for years. Fuck, I was hard solely from my thoughts steered that way. Maybe it was because I hadn't been laid in a while. Maybe it was because I was back in the same town with the woman I'd always wanted. But still could never have.

"No, really," he prodded. "What's the full story? I know there's a story."

"The story?" I set the clothes down again and stalked past Kennedy and into the temporary command center. We were all ready to get out of Gram's sewing room and into the new state-of-the-art building being built beside the bunkhouse. The floral wallpaper in here made me angry.

I couldn't talk about Indigo being naked when I was holding her bra and panties. "It was... nine years ago. Buck and I were home on leave. My grandparents were away, so we had a party in the back forty—where I'm building my cabin. I came inside and found Indi in my bed. Completely naked."

Kennedy whistled, eyebrows up. "How old was she?"

"Eighteen."

"Ripe and with her cherry?" Hayes piped in. "I bet—"

I shoved an office chair in Hayes' direction, and it went careening against his legs.

He stopped it but had to jump back. "What the fuck, man?"

"Don't talk about her cherry."

Kennedy grinned. "Did you pop it?"

I tossed my hands heavenward. "For fuck's sake! I didn't touch her. I covered my eyes and told her to get out. Then Buck showed up and nearly kicked my ass."

"Ah. So you wanted to tap it, but Buck cock-blocked you," Kennedy added.

"No!" I exploded.

It was a damn lie, but I wasn't going to give Kennedy any more ammunition. One look at Indi, all that creamy skin and guilelessness... yeah, and I'd wanted her. Hadn't wanted anyone else since. I'd had women, but Indi was the fucking prize. The one I knew once I sank balls deep into I'd never be able to survive. Maybe that was one of the reasons I avoided her now. She was the only thing left, the only person left on this fucking planet with the power to destroy me.

"I promised Buck I wouldn't touch her, and I won't. End of story."

"Right. Tell that story to your dick," Hayes said with a laugh, then hightailed it out of there before I could kill him.

CHAPTER
FIVE

INDI

AFTER THREE DAYS in the wilderness with three couples from Omaha, finalizing paperwork for the trip and putting equipment away, making chit-chat with Brandon was the last thing I wanted to do.

"I'm wiped. I'm headed home to get cleaned up and go to bed early."

I hadn't worn the same clothes for three days, but I was dusty, covered in sunscreen, and hadn't had more than a washcloth rinse-off in a creek in all that time. My hair was pulled back, but it was snarled and tangled. My mom had left a text the night I left to tell me she'd stuck a casserole in the freezer for me to heat up when I got home. The idea of her chicken enchiladas made my mouth water.

There were things that needed attention at Sparks Outdoor Adventure, but I could do them tomorrow. Or Brandon could take care of it since it was his company.

"There's a band playing at K-Sparks," he said, referring to the local radio station, KSPK, which doubled as a bar and outdoor music venue in the summer. "Want to meet me down there after you've had a shower?"

Ugh. I hated that he knew my routine. Ordinarily, I would've loved to head to K-Sparks after a long trek once I'd had time to shower, rest and recover. We used to meet there. As friends. After college, I'd thought I had the perfect job—a cool, laid-back boss with whom I was more friends than employee. One night, we hooked up. I'd been grieving Buck. Maybe I'd been a little lost. I'd also had a couple of beers.

I told him I didn't want a relationship, and he'd agreed it was just a no-strings kind of thing, but I should've known better. Because now he was what the movies called a Stage-5 Clinger. He kept trying to make it happen again, and I kept refusing. It was getting damned awkward.

"No, I'll stay in for the night," I said.

"Sure."

I took a step toward the door then turned back. I'd had so much time to think on this but had been afraid to say anything. But fuck it, since we were talking, I went for it. It couldn't go any worse than my talk the other day with Ford.

"Listen, Brandon."

He glanced up at me with a weird glint of hope in his dark eyes.

"I know you mentioned wanting to move back to Oregon. I was wondering if you'd consider selling SOA to me? You weren't going to take all the equipment with you, were you? I could, um, take over as the new owner. Keep your legacy going, you know?" I flashed him a smile meant to make him proud of what he'd created here, which, I had to be honest, was mostly my doing anyway. He wasn't the best at business, and he had no sense of direction, so he couldn't lead wilderness trips. He'd taken a day trip group intending to go to Elbow Lake and a fun little cave, but he'd ended up getting them lost, and Search and Rescue had been called in to get them.

Why he'd started an outdoor guide company, I had no idea. I didn't mention any of that because on top of not sleeping with him again, I didn't think he needed any more of an ego hit.

I wanted to buy his company not ride his dick.

"Oh." He shoved his fingers through his chin-length hair. I couldn't help but mentally compare him to Ford. Heck, even Kennedy. Those guys were men. Sturdy, solid, I won't-get-lost-in-the-woods men. "Well, I don't know when exactly I'm leaving, but yeah, I would consider it. Do you have a figure in mind?"

I did. I'd done some online research into selling businesses. I knew the approximate value of all the camping and hiking equipment, and I also had a pretty good estimate of the annual income of the place. Some businesses sold for three times their annual income, but I didn't think SOA was worth that much. I planned to offer somewhere between the capital equipment value and the annual income, but I wanted to see how much I could get in a loan.

"I do, but let me put it down on paper for you, okay? I want to be sure I've considered everything first."

"Yeah, okay." He nodded from behind the counter. "That sounds good."

For some reason, Brandon looked more bitter than excited.

Had he been bluffing about leaving town? Had

that been a threat meant to punish me for not wanting a relationship?

Ugh. Men! Why did it feel like I never could get it right with the opposite sex? The one I wanted didn't want me, and the one who wanted me I sure-as-hell didn't.

Nope. I wouldn't think of Ford. Not about his big, broad shoulders. Or the hungry way he looked at my body when I was soaked to the skin with rainwater. I'd felt more when he'd looked me over than when I'd been having sex with Brandon.

I wasn't sure if that said something about me, Ford, or Brandon.

"All right, see you tomorrow," I called, suddenly in even more of a hurry to get the hell out of there, to get away from those crazy thoughts.

I shook my head to clear it as I pulled out of the lot and headed toward my house. It wasn't far, thankfully. Nothing was in Sparks.

The days away should have erased Ford from my mind. I'd had to focus on the group of hikers I guided instead of Ford. Making sure they were happy. Had no blisters. Weren't hungry. Saw the elk grazing in the distance. Ensured all the food was in the hang bag away from bears.

I'd done all that but was still left with plenty of

free time for my mind to wander. To think about how much he'd changed. How angry he was. Just as focused as ever, but it seemed honed somehow, like a blade sharpened on a rock. I knew he was affected by Buck's death. The two of them had always been close. Closer than Buck and I, and he was my brother.

But Ford was also an asshole. I'd practically *given* myself to him, and he'd turned me away. Kicked me out of his bedroom—not before Buck had shown up.

I huffed out a breath as I slowed my old 4Runner around a turn. The usual thwump from the rotors was a reminder I needed to schedule a time for it to be worked on at Lee Lander's shop.

I had to get Ford out of my head because he was in there, running as if he were on a damned hamster wheel. He was trouble. Always had been. Not only did he remind me of Buck and the constant, numbing loss, but Ford made me feel inadequate. Less than. As if I'd never be enough for him. He'd never see me as anything more than his best friend's little sister.

At eighteen, I'd been daring and bold climbing into his bed. I still was when it came to anything but Ford Ledger. An hour with him during the storm the other day had validated every bit of insecurity I had and reinforced that Ford still had no interest.

I knew I shouldn't set my worth based on a man's opinion of me, but Ford...

"Let him go, Indi," I muttered to myself.

All I wanted to do now was strip out of my dirty clothes and take a long, hot shower. Eat the casserole that I didn't cook over a fire and sleep in an actual bed. I loved camping and loved being off the grid, but I enjoyed the comforts of civilization too.

The group I'd led had been really great. Eager for their vacation and easy going. They didn't complain about how soggy the ground was or that an animal had, sometime in the middle of the night, gotten into one of their packs and eaten all the snack bars they'd brought. Thankfully, not a bear.

Except they'd been a reminder that I wasn't part of a couple. That I didn't have a guy to climb into a tent with at night. That the only dick I was getting was made out of silicone and came with a charging cord.

A ten-mile hike to Messer Lake was tiring no matter how many times I'd been there, and I was ready for a few days off. My next scheduled trip, this time a white water rafting and camping combo, meant I'd be gone for a week.

My house was on the edge of town. It was nothing big, just a cute little rancher. My parents had given me the down payment for it a few months after Buck had died. When it had come on the market—after the elderly owner moved into assisted living—they'd thought it would be perfect for me. Perfect that they knew I would be living nearby, putting down roots in Sparks instead of going off and getting myself blown up.

I wasn't sure if the house purchase was for me or for them. It didn't really matter. Buck's death skewed everything about what was important. I never intended to leave Sparks, and I had only for college. I'd started to work for the wilderness company after graduation, and I'd been there ever since. My plan was to start my own business some-day, but I hadn't had the confidence to do it, espe-cially with Buck gone. He'd left for basic training when I was thirteen and had only been back on leave a few times in all the years since. I was used to him being away, but that was so much different than him being *gone.*

I turned down my street and blinked.

"What the hell?"

Two sheriff vehicles were in front of my house. I pulled into my short driveway and glanced around.

The last time I'd had contact with someone official was when they came to tell us about Buck.

"Oh my God." I hopped from my SUV like it was on fire and ran for the front door, my heart in my throat. Megan Hager, a sheriff deputy, stood there, hand resting on the butt of her gun, waiting for me.

"My parents? What's wrong?" I said, adrenaline pumping through my veins.

Megan raised her hand and offered a small smile. She stepped close, set that hand on my shoulder and met my eyes. She was the same height, so her dark gaze was direct.

"Your parents are fine."

I exhaled and felt like an empty balloon. I dropped onto the concrete stoop in relief. It was the middle of the day, and the neighborhood was quiet. Everyone was at work.

"Okay. Okay. Good." I set a hand on my chest and tried to calm down. I had no idea I could be so panicked, so fast.

She squatted in front of me in her crisp tan uniform. The walkie talkie on her hip beeped, and someone was talking, but the volume was too low for me to understand. Megan was a few years older than me, closer to Buck's age. She'd grown up in Sparks and only left town to go to the police academy in

Missoula before returning and joining the local sheriff's department. Every time I saw her, I thought she looked more like a model than a law enforcement officer, but she couldn't help that she was gorgeous. Bad guys must stop running away just to get her number.

"I'm sorry I scared you like that," she said, offering me a sympathetic smile. She was quiet for a moment, letting me settle. "We're here because your house was broken into."

I whipped my head around to my partially opened door. Now I noticed the damage to the door I'd painted red earlier in the summer and the frame. Beyond, my coffee table was upside down.

I popped to my feet and pushed the door open.

"Holy shit."

It was as if a hurricane had come through the inside of my house. Couch cushions strewn. Books on the floor. Kitchen cabinets opened. As I walked in, I could see through to my bedroom, and my clothes had been tossed.

"I'm guessing you were off on a guide trip," she said, her voice calm and even.

I nodded, staring at my desk. It was beneath the big bay window that looked out onto the street, the mountains in the distance. I loved the view.

My papers were everywhere. Drawers dumped on the carpet.

"Yeah," I said, taking it all in. "I've been gone a few days."

Another officer came out of my bathroom. "Hey, Indi."

It was Dan Murphy. Mid-thirties, had a wife and two kids. Coached the little league baseball team. I knew this about him, and they both knew about me, my job. Buck. About everything.

"Can you tell us if anything looks missing?" he asked.

I ran a hand over my scraggly hair. God, I was a mess and smelled.

I didn't care right about now.

Slowly I made my way through the house. It was a living room, dining room combo, but my desk took up that area. The kitchen was galley-style, and I couldn't go into it without stepping on a dish or strewn napkins or silverware.

I did a U-turn and went down the short hall to my bedroom. I didn't even enter because it was too destroyed. I turned around and peeked in the bathroom where my towels, medicine and toiletries were all over the tile.

"I don't have anything of much value," I said, walking back to the living room. They hadn't followed —because it would've been too crowded—and had been patient while I looked. I pointed to my desk. "My laptop's still there, but it's old and not worth anything. The same goes for my TV." I glanced to the older model that was a hand-me-down from my parents, which nobody would find of any value. It was also probably a hundred pounds. I wasn't around to watch it much.

"Prescription drugs?" Dan asked, scratching his head with the back of his pen.

"Like Oxy?" I asked, making sure he didn't want to know about birth control.

He nodded.

"Nope."

Dan jotted that down on his little notepad.

"How did you find out this happened?" I wondered.

"This morning, a neighbor was walking her dog and saw the door open. She knew you were away and called us in," Megan explained.

"Mrs. Schmit." The older woman took her miniature Schnauzer, Mitzi, for a walk around the block at seven every morning.

Megan nodded.

"She didn't see anything though? I mean, whoever did this?"

She shook her head. "No. We think it happened overnight, but we can't be sure since you've been gone."

"My mom texted yesterday morning, saying she stuck a casserole in my freezer. She would've called you if she found the place like this, so I think you're right," I surmised.

"Do you have a cat?"

I frowned. "No."

"Well, the door was open long enough for someone's cat to be inside. We shooed him—or her—out when we didn't see a litter box."

I closed my eyes for a second. "Were my parents called?"

Dan shook his head. "Not that we know of. We hadn't even had a chance to call you yet. I'm going to assume that since they're not here, they don't know about it."

"Yet," I added.

They were going to freak, and that was the last thing they needed.

"I'll call them," I said, not looking forward to telling them about this since I hated to upset them.

"Got any idea why someone would want to do this?" Dan asked.

I shook my head. I had no clue.

"What the fuck happened here?"

At the booming voice, all three of us whipped around toward the open front door. Dan pulled his gun from his holster, but lowered his hand when he saw who it was.

Ford practically filled the doorframe, all alpha lumberjack and fury while holding the clothes from the other day, panties and sports bra on top.

Megan eyed my underclothes then me. She gave me a look, but I wasn't in the mood to explain.

"I had a break-in," I said, stating the obvious.

Ford's long legs closed the distance between us in two long strides, and he tossed the clothes he'd held on the floor. He grabbed my arms and looked me over. "Are you hurt? Did they touch you?"

I blinked, stunned by his rage and the gentleness of his hold. Just like that, all my past pining for Ford—the gigantic crush I'd believed was true love—returned in a rush. It had been moments like this that had forged my attachment to him. He'd always been protective. Equally or more so than my own brother. When I was twelve, he'd carried me home from the park in his strong arms when I sprained an ankle. As the high school football star, he was already bulging with muscles and potent pheromones that worked their way into my senses and left me impossibly infatuated.

This moment was no different. His large hands were closed softly around my arms, his blue gaze filled with concern.

I cleared my throat. "I wasn't here." My voice came out sounding breathless. "I've been on a trip since Tuesday."

He sighed, took a moment to study me, then looked around. "Anything taken?"

"Not that I can tell."

"Hey, Ford," Dan said. "Didn't recognize you with the beard."

Ford ran his hand over it as if he'd just remembered it was there. "Dan, Megan." He nodded at the two law enforcement officers. "Got any idea what the fuck is going on here?"

Dan shook his head. "Like Indi said, nothing appears to be missing."

Ford glanced my way. "Cash?"

I thumbed over my shoulder. "Maybe a few dollars on my dresser in the bedroom, but I'm not rich."

They might not know my bank account balance,

but all three of them knew I worked as a wilderness guide and paid my own way. I wasn't rolling in money. Neither were my parents running a small-town hardware store.

Ford stepped back and set his hands on his hips. I could tell his mind was working, trying to assess the situation, figure out whatever it was skilled SEAL operatives worked through.

There was no enemy here, at least not any longer. No threat or danger.

"After you pick up, let us know if you find anything else missing," Megan said. "I'm sure your dad can fix the lock—"

"I'll fix the lock," Ford cut in.

My parents were known to tackle things like this. Installing new locks, making replacement keys.

But Ford?

"And install a security system," he added. "But she's not staying here."

My eyes widened. "This is my house. I'm staying—"

"With me," he finished.

I set my hands on my hips and squared off with him. "Uh uh. Ford, you can't boss—"

I saw Megan hide a smile. She was probably assuming far more was going on between me and

Ford than was the case. Especially since he came in with my clothes and underwear in plain sight.

"Once your parents hear about this, you're going to be in your old bedroom before sundown," Ford said. "I doubt they'll let you back here to live by yourself until not only new locks are put on, but their nerves are under control. That could be weeks."

I opened my mouth to argue, but he was right. He knew my parents as well as I did. Lord knew, they'd been like replacement parents to him since he didn't have his own. My parents would panic.

"You'll stay with me where it's fucking safe, and I can keep an eye on you."

"An eye on me?" I moved to stand right in front of him, tipping my head back to give him every bit of defiance. "An *eye* on me? This alpha protective thing you've got going on is great and all, but I can take care of myself. I wasn't even here. I was up at Messer Lake, miles away."

Ford shook his head. "Yeah, telling me you were out in the wilderness alone isn't a comfort, Blue. I need to know you're safe."

My heart flip-flopped again at his use of his pet name for me.

"I wasn't alone."

"You were the other day."

"I was out *hiking*. For fun," I countered.

"When did you two start dating?" Dan asked.

Ford and I turned our heads to stare at him.

"What?" Ford asked.

"We're not dating," I said at the same time.

Dan laughed. "*Right.* Okay, so we'll just leave you guys to this," he said. "Stop by the station tomorrow to sign some papers, okay, Indigo?"

I mustered a smile for him and Megan. "Thanks for being here and checking it out. I'll call my dad and get the new door lock."

They eyed us, probably wondering if they'd be back for a domestic dispute call, then left, pulling the front door closed as best as they could on the way.

"It's your parents or me until we know what's going on. Why someone broke in. Until then, it's not smart to be here. The door doesn't close well." He stepped close and used his size to loom. The fucker. "They might come back, Indi."

Come back? They didn't take anything the first time, so why would they do that?

Still, I didn't like the idea of being here when... *if* that happened. I wasn't sure if it was lucky I hadn't been home.

"I'll sleep in my tent."

"You'd rather sleep in a fucking tent than stay with me?"

I pursed my lips. "Ford, I'm not staying with you. And Kennedy and the other guys. And your grandmother."

"Fine." He glanced around. "Then I'm staying here with you."

"We're not even friends."

For some reason, Ford flinched at that, and some of my resentment toward him fell away. Maybe he'd avoided us since he'd been back for the same reason my parents avoided him. It was too painful to be around people who reminded us of Buck.

"We're family, Indi."

I put my hands on my hips. "No, we're not. And I don't need a replacement big brother, so stop acting like one."

He stared at me for a beat. "My last promise to Buck was to keep you safe. Don't make it hard for me to keep that promise." His voice was still deep and rough, but I heard pain in it.

That knocked the breath out of me.

"Buck asked you to look after me?" Sadness enveloped me, thinking of my overprotective, bossy older brother. I was...deeply touched. To think he'd cared that much about me to have had me on his mind even overseas. My eyes stung.

"My place or I stay here."

"Fine. Here."

I didn't want to go back to my parents' house, and Ford was right. Once they heard about this and saw the mess that had been made, they'd take me home, feed me meatloaf and mashed potatoes, wrap me in bubble wrap and lock me in my room. I didn't want to go with Ford either. But I also didn't want to stay without locks that worked. Having Ford here would ensure my safety.

Although I doubted how safe my pride would be with him. Because for some reason an angry and growly Ford made me wet. Horny. I did like him being all protective. To know that I wasn't alone. That he'd keep me safe.

Every one of those thoughts was stupid. Because I wanted him, and that was that dumbest thing of all.

"I need a shower," I said. "But I need to call my parents before they find out about the break-in through the Sparks gossip mill."

He looked me over again, and my body heated. Stupid body.

"You shower. I'll call Kennedy to bring a new lock and install a security system."

"A *security system?*"

He continued to eye me in a way that said he wasn't changing his mind.

"Fine. But you're still not my big brother," I called out as I clomped to the bathroom, cell in hand.

"Well aware," I heard him mutter just before I shut the door.

CHAPTER
SIX

FORD

MY FEELINGS *for you are far from brotherly, Blue.*

I rubbed my forehead as I stared at the closed bathroom door, listening to the sound of the shower.

I had a hard-on knowing Indi was naked beyond that door. I didn't need a woman with makeup and heels to be turned on. It seemed my dick liked a woman dusty and trail worn. Or it just wanted Indi.

To distract myself, I took a slow tour around the room. I would help her clean up the mess, but first I wanted to take things in the way they were. Someone had been looking for something. That was the part that made me uneasy. Had they found what they'd been looking for? No laptop was taken. No TV missing although no one would want that old thing. What worried me was that they might come back to keep looking. But who would want anything from Indi? Like she'd said, she and her family weren't made of money, and Buck hadn't received any death benefits from the military.

I would ask her about who she worked and hung out with. She didn't like to share shit with me. Hell, I probably would have never known about the break-in until Gram heard the gossip and shared if I hadn't seen the cop cars parked out front.

I couldn't let this go. Someone broke *into her house*. In Sparks. *Nothing* happened in this town. I'd do whatever necessary to keep her safe, including taking out anyone who was fucking with her. I'd turn it into an interrogation if need be.

It was my job to keep her safe, and I'd blown it. I'd had my head up my ass while someone rifled through her panty drawer.

Thank fuck she'd been on a guide trip and not here—but still. I ran a fucking security company, and I couldn't keep Indi safe. Why hadn't I thought to secure her house? I pulled out my cell and texted Kennedy.

I need a new door lock dropped off and a full security treatment on Indi's house. Top priority tomorrow.

By the time Kennedy was done, we'd know if an ant came in for a bread crumb.

In the meantime, no one was getting to Indi without getting through me first.

Pissed, I went into her bedroom, looking at the emptied dresser drawers. All the pictures hung askew on the walls, like the fuckers had looked behind each one.

A scarf pinned to the wall had been half torn down. I walked over because it was obviously a screen for something else. A bulletin board.

I removed the fabric and took in everything that was tacked to the corkboard. The letter from the Navy telling of Buck's death. Another one with the official finding that Buck had been found guilty—posthumously—of murder. A highlighter had been used to circle the name of the signatory. James Knighton. A half-dozen index cards were pinned to the board. One had the name of the village where Buck had been killed. One had Sergeant Major Johnson, the commanding officer of the Ranger Beta Team he'd been pulled onto. Another had my name and Lincoln's, my commanding officer. Huh. She had William Gentry, the translator Buck had replaced—

the one Kennedy just found out had committed suicide recently. That one made ice sluice through my veins.

How much had Indi been poking into this case? I knew my efforts had certainly caused a ripple in the military. A ripple big enough to get me dismissed. Was it possible this break-in was related to Buck's case? Had she stirred the pot enough somehow to get someone's attention to come here and search the place? Had they seen this board?

Why her? Why now? If someone was doing surveillance, why not me? I was the one who'd obviously been pushing for the truth. This board meant Indi was curious, but how would anyone know she had it? The fuckers were well-connected and had enough clout to frame Buck. Kick me out of the Navy.

But Indi was completely innocent, and that made me really fucking nervous. Besides Kennedy doing the security install, I'd get him working for intel, too.

"What are you doing in here?" Indi's voice wavered, starting off bold but dropping a little when she saw what I was looking at. Yeah, she knew she was in fucking trouble. Poking around in shit she shouldn't. She stood in nothing but a goddamn

towel, which didn't help with my unbrotherly feelings or my brain processing since my blood was
moving south to my dick. Why was she always
barely dressed and dripping wet?

I gritted my teeth.

"What the hell is this?" I pointed at the board.

"Nothing." She stomped into the room, then
faltered when she turned to the dresser and was
reminded her clothing wouldn't be easy to find.

If I were a gentleman, I'd leave, so she could get
dressed.

I usually was a gentleman, but not in this case.
Indi wasn't a lady, she was... Indigo, the bright,
familiar, gorgeous sister of my dead best friend. One
who was smart enough to know that nothing about
Buck's death rang true. Because she had a fucking
bulletin board about it.

It wasn't safe for her to be looking into this. Not
at all. Not when two people had already been killed,
not that I was going to tell her that.

"What is this about?" I asked gruffly. I didn't like
it. She shouldn't be nosing around in it–whatever
was going on was big. And dangerous.

She was a wilderness guide who'd barely left the
state. She had *zero* clue. I wanted to spank her ass for

endangering herself and protect her at the same time. The only place I knew she was truly safe was in my arms. Keeping her out of them was now impossible.

Someone had broken into her house. She was snooping into shit she had no idea how dangerous it really was. Hell, I didn't either.

"It doesn't matter. There's nothing there. I made it because I needed to understand, but there's nothing to figure out. It's all a dead end." She put her hands on her hips, which was a big mistake because the fucking towel flapped open.

I didn't know why I rushed to help her with it. With a damned yellow towel. She didn't need me closer. She needed me farther away. Out of her bedroom.

You touch Indigo, and I will cut your nuts off.

That had been Buck's warning to me after he'd caught us in my room that night.

But here I was, one hand on each corner of the towel, pulling it open to make the terry cloth taut.

"*Ford.*" Indi's startled gaze locked onto mine. Her full lips parted in surprise. I quickly wrapped the towel back around her and tucked the edges, my fingers brushing over her damp skin just above her breasts.

Not quickly enough, though.

I'd had the misfortune of seeing all of Indi's glorious and fully naked form before I managed to get her covered again. Except, who was I kidding? There was no universe where seeing Indigo Buchanan naked could be considered a misfortune.

My throbbing dick was a testament to that fact.

I'd wanted her when she was eighteen. Lusted after her hot body. Even with a second's glance, I'd just seen she was still perfect. Her hips had filled out. So had her tits. All woman.

"Sorry," I said gruffly, not meaning a fucking syllable. But I didn't let go. I didn't know what was wrong with me, but I couldn't seem to step back. Couldn't seem to relinquish control of her towel. Or hide my heated gaze. Maybe it was the strawberry scent of her shampoo.

"Don't—" She licked her lips and glanced at my shirt, at the floor. "Don't pretend you find me attractive. We both know it's not true."

I stilled. Processed. *What the actual fuck?*

"You've got to be fucking kidding me." My eyes popped wide. "Is that what you think? Seriously?"

She tried to pull back, and I was an even bigger asshole because I kept my fingers curled into the top of her towel. The soft swells of her breasts were against my knuckles.

There was no way I was letting her go now. Not until she knew exactly how far from the truth that statement was.

"Indigo, are you nuts?"

Her nostrils flared like she was about to get pissed off again, but this time I didn't encourage it. This time I saw the hurt behind her anger, and it seemed important that I correct her notion.

"You've been a goddamn torment to me," I blurted.

She went still and finally lifted her chin, her blue eyes wide on mine.

I saw into them. All the hurt. All the sadness. All the desire.

"You're... That night... Of course, I find you—" Fuck it. I was never great with words. I had to show her. Make her believe.

My mouth stamped over hers, my tongue swept between her lips. Still holding the front of her towel with one hand, I cradled her head with the other and kissed the hell out of Indigo Buchanan with a full-on, no holds barred assault. Then I changed the angle and kissed her harder. Made her feel all the frustrated, pent-up passion I'd had simmering for her for years.

Years.

"Now, you tell me," I said, breaking the kiss abruptly, leaving her gasping, her cheeks flushed. My dick was achingly hard as I rolled my hips against her. "Do you think I find you attractive?"

Indi did the worst thing imaginable. She teared up.

Then she slapped me.

I took the hit and felt the blunt sting. That finally shook some sense into me, and I released her, taking a step back.

"Sorry," I said quickly. "I'm sorry, Indi. I didn't—"

Then she came rushing back, her arms around my neck as she did the assaulting this time. The towel fell away, and I had Indi's soft, naked form pressed against mine. My arms went around her, feeling the silky skin of her back, the full globes of her perfect ass.

"Fuck," I cursed, not even sure how I'd gotten myself here.

How I'd broken my vow to Buck. Because my hands were all fucking over her.

It didn't matter. There was no way in hell I'd

reject Indi again. Not when she showed me her vulnerability like that. Showed me that I was the reason she thought, even for one second, she wasn't perfect. Wasn't worthy. Shit, I hadn't even known it, but I'd hurt her. She'd assumed I didn't want her when that was the furthest thing from the truth.

If Buck were here, he'd kick my ass, but I'd take it. It'd be worth it.

"Beautiful," I panted between hot kisses, my hands continuing to roam down the slope of her back. "You're so fucking beautiful." I squeezed her ass, lifting her hips to rub over mine.

She slid her hands up under my t-shirt, and I took her cue. I yanked it over my head and tossed it into the heap of clothing that littered the floor.

I caught her deer-in-the-headlights look as she took in my torso and slowed the fuck down. Aw, shit. She couldn't still be a virgin, could she? No. There was no way. This body, this woman, not passionate?

"Wait—am I going too fast?" I asked.

She let out a scoff. "I'm not a virgin, Ford."

Right. She'd offered me that part of her, and I'd refused it. She'd given it to someone else, and it was totally my fucking loss.

"We don't have to do this. Fuck—we shouldn't do this."

But then her piss and vinegar returned. "I'm naked before you. Again. Don't you dare make me feel like a slut again, Ford Ledger."

"*Slut?*" I echoed in shock. "Are you fucking kidding me?" I was pissed now but only at myself. Because it seemed she believed I didn't want her, *and* I thought her a slut? That was so fucked up, which meant I'd done a number on her.

"Christ, I never meant to make you feel that way." I reached for her. "Come here," I said, trying to soften my voice. "No wonder you hate me."

"I do," she muttered but allowed me to pull her back into my arms. Let me stroke her damp hair away from her face. "I've hated you since that night. You ruined my sex life."

"No," I groaned. The need to fix this, to mend what I'd broken, burned my already tattered resolve about not breaking my promise to Buck. I cradled one side of her face and brushed her cheek with my thumb. "You're perfect. You were then. So brave. You are now. Let me show you." I dipped my head to kiss her again, slowly this time. As I moved my lips across hers, I backed her toward the bed.

When her legs hit the mattress, I gently pushed her hips down and knelt between her knees.

"Can I show you?" My voice was rough with desire.

She held my gaze as I spread her wide. Her blue eyes were dark with heat, but she still seemed unsure. I hated that she didn't trust me.

"We shouldn't," she murmured. "You said—"

"You're right. We shouldn't. You think I hate you. I don't. Fuck, no. If I ruined your sex life because of that night, then it's my job to fix it." I took in her perfect, pink pussy and groaned. She wasn't waxed bare like some women. The brown hair there was trimmed short and neat. Thank fuck because I was hard for the grown-up Indi. The *woman*. "I'm supposed to take care of you. Whatever you need. And by the way your pussy's dripping, it needs to come."

Her head fell back on the messy bed, and she stared up at the ceiling. "Ford," she whispered.

My palms slid up her silky thighs, and she didn't stop me. Her skin was so soft and delicate, but the toned muscles beneath reminded me of her strength and power.

"I need a yes, Blue."

I stopped my fingers just short of her center and waited. She hated me. She'd just slapped me, and I was about to eat her pussy and get her to come all over my face.

I needed her consent. I was about to pull my hands away when she finally nodded and whispered, "Yes."

Fuck me. She said yes. My mouth watered, and I wasn't waiting a second longer to taste her. To make her mine. Yeah, fucking make her mine because if she thought I'd ever let another man get in this spot, see her open and perfect like this...

Hell no.

I'd kill them. And I'd been trained for years on how to do that.

I even knew how to make the body disappear.

I pushed her knees wider and lowered my head, used my thumbs to spread her open, and licked into her. She gasped the moment my tongue parted her sweet flesh, her knees clapping against my ears.

One sweet taste, one sugary whiff, and I was ruined. It was as if she was imprinted, embedded now in my DNA. If she thought I was a bossy, protective asshole before... now?

This pussy was M.I.N.E.

Yeah, Buck would have my dick for this if he were alive, but this moment was destined. She needed me to watch out for her. To give her the pleasure her body deserved. To pull out the true, real Indigo Buchanan and make her come. Make her writhe with passion.

To complete her.

The task made my dick pulse, spurt pre-cum in my jeans. My balls ached, and all I wanted to do was sink into her. Except my dick wasn't in charge here. It would have to fucking wait.

Indi came first.

I wouldn't tease her, but I'd take my time. Licking and flicking, watching her responses. Learning the amount of pressure that made her clench, the exact spots that made her gasp. Then I added my fingers to the party and circled her weeping entrance, then slid them inside. Fuck, she was tight and hot. I still watched her, looking up her perfect body, past those pert breasts and tight nipples to see her mouth open, her head thrash on her bed.

When she called out my name and clenched down on my fingers, I knew I'd found her g-spot. I curled them and flicked the left side of her swollen clit.

"There," she breathed.

That was my girl. Fuck, yes. "That's right. Tell me what you want."

"Stop talking," she snapped and used her knees to pull me back into place.

"Yes, ma'am," I breathed, then set upon my task again.

I was going to be smothered by her pussy, but what a fucking way to go. One thing a military man was good at was taking orders.

I flicked and curled, stroked and sucked until she coiled and coiled and then exploded.

She moaned and arched her back, her pussy clenching and milking my fingers. A hot gush of arousal made her slick, my palm wet. My beard was coated.

I kissed her thigh, then worked my way up her body. I couldn't help the smirk as I hovered over her, seeing her flushed and sated, eyes closed. Yeah, I'd made her this way.

"I've never come with a guy before," she admitted.

My smile dropped. I wanted to hunt every one of those assholes down and murder them for getting their hands on Indi and treating her wrong. Leaving her hanging was a crime. I also didn't even want to think about the fact that I'd been offered this... and I'd turned my back on it.

But I was also laced with determination. Because

the only man who'd satisfied her was me. Was *going* to be me.

"That's number one," I said. "The next time you come is going to be all over my dick."

She looked up at me then. "I want to see you. I want—" Biting her lip, she stifled the rest of her words. The flush grew brighter on her cheeks and spread down her neck. Her gaze flicked away.

Christ. She may not be a virgin, but she wasn't exactly free with her sexuality.

I plucked that plump bottom lip from her teeth with my thumb. "You don't have to hide from me. What you want. Tell me." She stayed quiet, and I cupped her cheek and made her look at me. "Tell me," I repeated.

"Gah."

"Say it."

"I can't."

"Why not?"

"I don't know. I'm not a slut, okay?"

Damn. There was that word again. I couldn't believe I'd made her feel that way. I wanted to punch my own face.

"Slut? For telling your lover what makes you hot?"

She nodded against my palm.

"Nothing, and I mean *nothing,* you could ever want sexually would turn me off." I leaned down and kissed the tip of her nose. "You can be *my* little slut if that makes you feel better."

The corner of her mouth tipped up. Bracing on one hand by her head, I reached down and opened my jeans, pushed them and my boxers down enough so my dick sprang free.

She looked down between us to it.

"Nothing," I said again, gripping the base and giving my hard length a pump. A bead of pre-cum oozed from the tip.

"Let me up," she whispered.

Fuck, I'd messed up. I pushed off the bed and sat back on my heels. She met my gaze and slowly rolled over onto her stomach. She wasn't getting out of bed and ending this. Hell no. She was coming up onto her hands and knees then dropping to her fore-arms. From my position, her ass was right fucking there. So was her pussy and... fuck *me.*

I growled, and she looked over her shoulder at me.

I couldn't resist running my hand over her ass, cupping that taut flesh. Eyeing that pink, swollen and slick flesh I'd just tasted.

"You wanna be fucked from behind?" I asked.

She bit her lip and nodded. This time when she did it, it was sultry and the sight of her would be something I'd *never* forget.

"You are such a good girl. Fuck, so perfect."

I came up on my knees, fished my wallet out of my back pocket, and grabbed a condom. I had no idea why I kept one in there because I hadn't gotten laid in forever, but I always had one out of habit. Prepared for any situation.

I couldn't take another second to shuck out of the rest of my clothes. Indi was primed and eager to be fucked. I'd deny her nothing.

So I rolled the condom on and gripped my dick, rubbing the head through her folds, coating the tip in all that sweet honey. She watched, wiggling her hips.

I spanked her ass, my handprint instantly appearing on that jiggling flesh.

She gasped, clearly surprised. I doubted she'd ever been spanked before. The way she pushed back, it turned out, it was something she liked.

"You're a good girl for showing me how you want to get fucked," I said.

I slid into her, one long stroke and groaned, low and deep.

Her walls clenched and adjusted to me. I wasn't

small, and she was tight as hell. I leaned over her, set my hand by her head again. I remained still, giving her a second to adjust.

Sweat beaded on my brow. She felt too good. Too perfect. Like I could die here and now.

I wasn't going to last long because she was just too amazing. My balls were drawn up, and I wanted to fill her and mark her inside and out. I'd protect her with the condom.

"Ford," she begged, moving forward and back and trying to fuck herself on me.

"So greedy," I replied, pulling almost all the way out. I slammed into her.

"Yes!"

I pulled back again. "Look at you, on your hands and knees taking my dick," I murmured, my mouth by her ear. I fucked her hard again. I felt her get wetter around me, learned she liked dirty talk.

She *was* a little slut, wild and passionate. But she was *my* little slut, and I wouldn't have her any other way. I wanted her uninhibited. Unbridled. Getting exactly what she needed sexually because I had a feeling it was going to match my needs.

"You liked that spanking? Maybe I'll take you over my knee and give you a real one."

"Ford," she moaned.

Yeah, I was pushing it, but I was inside Indi. I wanted every part of her. Every dark and naughty corner. She'd give me everything.

"Upturned asses get spanked," I said, rolling my hips to fuck her good. "And filled. At first it'll be my thumb in that virgin hole. Then sometime soon my dick."

"Oh my God," she whimpered and clenched around me.

I grinned then realized I had to get her to come again. Now. Because she was into what I'd just said, and the thought of taking her ass was going to have me blow.

I pushed off, wrapped my arm around her waist, and pulled her up so she was sitting on my thighs. One hand cupped her breast and plucked the taut little nipple. My other slid down her body and found where we were joined. Felt her lips wrapped around my dick as I moved in and out of her. Then I pinched her clit, tugged on it.

"Come for me, Blue. Come all over me."

I pumped into her, pushing her over the edge with a clench and a gush.

She screamed, a wild thing in my arms as she obeyed.

I didn't last one thrust before I filled her, held myself deep and let go.

Gave over to the sheer bliss that made me blind. Made me fucking forget my own name. Maybe it was a good thing I never fucked her that night long ago because if I had, I'd have gone AWOL and never returned.

I hadn't been ready for Indigo Buchanan, but I sure as shit was now.

CHAPTER
SEVEN

INDI

WHOA. *Wow.*

I couldn't believe I just had sex with Ford Ledger. Subject of all my teen fantasies then later—after *the incident*—all my hurt, anger and resentment.

The sex had been... explosive. Incredible. Satisfying times a gazillion. Clearly, that was how sex was supposed to be. It had been so different from my previous repressed attempts that they were now laughable.

He eased out of me and went to dispose of the condom and came back with a hand towel, wiping his beard, then his hands. As I absorbed what just happened—remembering the reason why he needed to wipe his face—uncertainty and a touch of shame crept back in. What would Buck have said about this? About me throwing myself at his best friend... again?

And what did it mean to Ford? Probably nothing.

Oh, God.

I scrambled to try to hunt for some clothes in the mess on the floor.

"Hold up," Ford barked in that gruff, bossy voice of his. The one that raised my hackles even after the incredible orgasms. Yeah, multiple orgasms.

Instead of facing off, though, I frantically sorted through the clothes trying to find something to wear.

"Indi."

I ignored him. Gah. This was just as humiliating as being naked in his bedroom all those years ago. When he'd covered his eyes, turned his back, and told me to get out. I'd rolled over, stuck my ass in the air, and all but told him to fuck me from behind.

Back then, he and Buck had been home on leave, and I'd just graduated high school. He'd been so friendly with me. By then, I wasn't the annoying kid sister. That week, we'd laughed and talked the night my parents had him over for dinner. I'd grown up, and I was sure he'd noticed. He hadn't been hitting on me, but I'd sensed his appreciation. His recognition that I was an adult—his equal. We'd laughed and joked together like old friends.

When he told me they were having a get-together with their old friends from high school, I'd thought the invitation meant something, that he'd really wanted me there. I hadn't guessed it had been a second-hand invite. The kind made to make people feel included and nothing more.

So I, living in my fantasy world, had bypassed the party down by the creek and went inside the house and up to his bedroom. I'd taken off my clothes to show him I was willing, that I knew what sailors wanted when they were home on leave.

I stupidly thought I'd be fulfilling his fantasies along with mine.

God, what an idiot I'd been!

"*Indigo.*" Ford caught me around the waist and pulled my back up against his front. I could feel how much bigger he was. How strong. How hard... everywhere. "What just happened? Why are you freaking out?"

"I'm not freaking out," I snapped, shutting my eyes. "I'm just trying to get dressed."

"Hang on, Blue." His lips found the place where my neck met shoulder, and he kissed me.

It was enough to calm the flutters in my belly. I relaxed a measure.

"Are you... ashamed... about what we did?" he murmured.

I went rigid again, and my eyes popped open, taking in the mess strewn all over the floor. "Of course not!" It was a lie. There was shame swirling around my chest, right along with the insecurity and fear of rejection. It was like I was eighteen again and bracing for Ford to cover his eyes and tell me to get out.

Except he didn't let me go. Instead, he loosened his hold and turned me in his arms. "I really fucked with your head, didn't I?" His blue eyes searched mine. Gone was the heat of desire, but I didn't see the usual hostility I'd thought he felt toward me. Instead, he'd been fighting his attraction.

Still, his balls were empty. He got off. He hadn't even gotten his pants to the floor. He could zip them back up and be on his way.

Except for once, his voice wasn't gruff or commanding. It was soft with regret. He wasn't mad. He appeared... shameful.

And with his question, all my defenses came

down. My muscles went lax in his hold. I nodded, tears threatening. "You and Buck both," I admitted.

His brows slammed down, and the tips of his fingers pressed into my skin. "What did Buck do?"

I tried to pull away, and Ford eased his grip. I didn't want to look him in the face when I talked about it. It was too embedded in humiliation for me. I went back to searching the floor for a clean pair of panties. "The day after the party, he came into my room and gave me a big lecture."

I finally found the pile of underwear. I selected a pair, then, thinking about my hot self-appointed bodyguard, changed my mind and selected a prettier pair—red with red lace.

Ford growled a little as I put them on, stepping up behind me to mold his hands around my asscheeks. "I like your panties," he murmured.

I turned to face him, and for the first time, I really drank him in. The new lines on his face. The beard. The haunted quality behind his eyes, even though he was sated from sex. I'd found his all-American good looks intoxicating before, but this rougher, worn version of him? It went straight to my heart. Because he'd lived through war. Through seeing his best friend die. Other things I knew he'd never be able to tell.

"Buck's the one who called me a slut," I told him. "Even though I'd been a virgin."

Ford winced. "I would fucking punch his teeth in if he were alive."

I let out a pained laugh and paced away from Ford again to locate the matching bralette. "He said he was ashamed of me for offering myself like that. I'd embarrassed myself in front of you, he scolded." It was easier to tell the story with my back turned. "I'd acted like a slut, and if I behaved like that with any other guys in town, I'd get a reputation." I located the bralette beneath a sweatshirt and pulled it over my head, adjusted it into place. "He didn't want my name—our name—to get sullied or some such bullshit."

"That *is* bullshit. Total bullshit." Ford sounded angry. He was in nothing but his jeans, the zipper up but the button was undone. It was his turn to pace around my room. "Indi..." He scrubbed a hand over his beard. "I'm sure Buck was trying to look out for you. He only said those stupid things because he cared and was trying to protect you when he couldn't be here to punch guys' faces in if they ever said something about you. Or tried anything."

I dismissed his words with a shrug.

"Like I said, it wasn't like I'd worked my way

through the football team my senior year. I wanted *you*. I'd think Buck would have been cool with it, but he lost his shit."

"He couldn't protect you any other time, so he went all out then." His words made sense, and I could tell he was trying to defend Buck. At least help me get his perspective. "That still didn't make it right."

I drew in a long breath and sigh. "Yeah." I found a soft t-shirt and pulled it on.

He cornered me again, his hands coming to lightly rest on my waist. "I'm sorry. When I found you in my room that night, I choked. You looked...so. Fucking. Amazing. Like an angel had dropped off my dream girl wrapped up in nothing but a bow. I hadn't even admitted to myself until that moment how hot I was for you, and there you were—giving me a Washington Monument-sized boner."

I couldn't help but laugh at that imagery.

"But what could I do?" he continued. "You saw him. I knew Buck would kill me if I touched you. I mean, seriously kick my ass. Fucking little sisters goes against every bro-code."

I lifted my chin, not too thrilled about the *whole bros before hoes scenario*. "So you picked humiliating me over standing up to Buck."

He winced again, sniffed and stroked his beard. I was recognizing it was his habit when frustrated. "At the time, I thought I was doing the right thing. I was only there for a week, and it couldn't have been anything more than that one time. We were sent off on missions, one after another. Bad shit. I thought I was protecting you. From me."

"What do you think now?" I asked, cocking my head.

"If I'd known I was damaging you, I would've tossed my buddy out the upstairs window before I let him cloud my judgment or call you a slut."

It was my turn to wince at the word. It still hurt.

Seeing my pain, Ford pulled me closer, and I felt good in his arms. "Slut is one of those words you have to take back," he murmured.

Take back?

I met his gaze and raised my brows. "You mean embrace it, so it doesn't hurt any longer? Now you *want* me to be a slut?"

His grin turned feral. He pointed at his chest. "*My* slut. As I said, whatever you need sexually, I'll give it to you. No holds barred. No shame."

A laugh tumbled from my lips, and I tried to ignore the fizzing and popping of excitement his words induced. At how I'd been bold and rolled onto all fours, so he could fuck me from behind. I hadn't expected him to spank my ass and talk dirty. So fucking dirty.

I'd liked it. All of it, and I hadn't felt slutty. Okay, maybe I had, a little. But with Ford? *For* Ford? It wasn't the same thing at all.

I couldn't trust in this, could I? That my teen crush actually wanted me now? That this was more than a just a quick fuck to... scratch an itch?

My phone rang from the living room. "I'd better get that. It's probably my parents again," I murmured, and Ford released me. I'd texted my mom to give her a heads up about the break-in so she didn't panic, and she was now getting back to me.

"Yeah," he said, pulling on his t-shirt. "I'll start cleaning up the mess."

I found my phone still in my backpack by the door, and I answered it.

"Indigo! I just heard." Yep, it was my mom.

"It's okay, Mom. Nothing's missing, and... Ford is here to fix my locks."

"Ford?" my mom echoed. It was like his name instantly calmed her but also pulled out her sadness.

I knew the feeling. Ford was so closely associated in all of our minds with Buck that it was hard to even think about him without the pain of Buck's death nearly splitting me open.

Just seeing Ford's truck around town would make me change my plans to avoid bumping into him.

"Yeah, he, um, saw the sheriff's car and stopped in to make sure I was okay. He's going to fix everything up and stay here with me until he's sure I'm safe."

"Stay there? Oh." My mom sounded confused, and who could blame her? It wasn't like Ford and I were even friendly a week ago. Not even an hour ago.

I heard him moving around behind me, picking up fallen furniture and straightening things. I shot him a glance and found him watching me. There was tension in his face like my mom had the same effect on him that he had on her. He didn't show tons of emotions, but I was starting to see the differences between his moody, intense looks. Protective Ford. Angry Ford. Sad Ford. Aroused Ford. Those emotions all looked the same on him... almost.

It made sense. We all suffered a loss with Buck's death. Maybe Ford even more than the rest of us— he'd been there when it happened.

"Yes," I continued. "He's concerned like you are. I'm sure it's fine, but he's playing big brother."

I immediately wished I hadn't said that. We'd just crossed over from him being replacement big brother to something else, and I very much preferred the something else. My pussy still throbbed from him being inside me.

Ford frowned like he didn't like it either.

"Well, I'm glad he's there," my mom said, still sounding slightly bewildered. "He's going to stay? With you?"

"Yes. Until he's sure I'm safe."

"Okay." I heard her exhale. "I trust him. He'll know what to do."

I watched Ford moving about the small house, his muscles bulging when he picked up the end of my couch to move it back to where it belonged. He was fierce and capable. Pushy and protective and possessive. For the first time in a while, I felt... something. And that was saying a lot.

"Yes," I agreed. "He will."

In so many ways.

CHAPTER
EIGHT

FORD

MY HONOR MAY HAVE BEEN TATTERED over my broken vow to Buck, but now there was no going back. Now that I'd tasted Indi, now that she'd been vulnerable with me—showed me the pain I'd caused—I wouldn't change it for the world.

Indigo was mine now. She belonged to me whether she realized it yet or not.

We hadn't gotten far on the clean-up yesterday as I'd pulled her back to bed and kept her there. Now, in the early morning light, I stalked around her place, examining everything before I put it to rights. Trying to figure out who the fuck would do this. And why.

I found myself back in her bedroom, staring at that bulletin board as if drawn to it. My life now was based on seeking the truth... and vengeance. This board called to me and scared the shit out of me.

I pulled all the pins out and took down the papers. "What are you doing?" she demanded. Her hair was mussed from a night of fucking. She was no longer naked—which was a shame—and in a pair of jeans and a pale blue top. Her feet were bare.

"This isn't healthy." I pointed at the board. That may or may not be the truth, especially when I was fixated on the exact same thing. Enough that I had three team members helping me investigate it all. But we were SEALs, not a one hundred pound wilderness guide.

The fact that her house had been broken into had me on edge. If it was related, she was in real danger.

But I wasn't going to tell her the real reason–that it wasn't safe for her to be looking at this board. Hell, even thinking about this shit. She'd maybe poked a fucking hornet's nest.

"Who are you to decide what's healthy and

what's not?" She tried to snatch the papers out of my hand, but I jerked them out of reach, demonstrating our size difference.

"Listen, Blue. Buck's gone. Nothing we do will bring him back." I hated saying those words, and they came out through gritted teeth, but they were fucking real. "I think the murder charge was bullshit, but you won't get anywhere barking up that tree. We'll never know the truth. It's the fucking military you're up against."

She folded her arms across her chest and narrowed her gaze at me. "Was it bullshit, Ford?"

Aw, fuck. I wanted to tell her the truth. I did. That I was going to clear Buck's name, to return the honor he wore like a fucking cape. I needed him to rest in peace. So I could be at peace too. Maybe.

The truth was going to spur on her search, though, same as it did mine. I couldn't have Indi looking into this. Buck had gotten killed over it, pinned for a murder I was sure he didn't commit. The other translator was killed or had killed himself, and it was made to look that way, based on what Kennedy'd been digging up. If Lincoln fed him that intel, then it was valid. Something he needed us to look into outside of military channels.

Whatever or whoever was behind Buck's death

and framing was big. Big enough to get me dismissed when I tried looking into it.

Certainly big enough to cause Indi harm if she got in the way.

Someone may have come out here to search her house to make sure she didn't know anything. It was that possibility—my fear that this break-in might somehow be related—that made me twist the truth.

I didn't want lies between us, but I had no choice. I'd protect her. No matter what.

"He left base without authorization and was in an area we weren't allowed to be in. It got him killed. I wish to God he'd gone out some other way because he was a goddamn hero, but the facts are facts. We can't change them."

Stubbornness warred with pain in her expression.

"And the murder charge?"

Fuck, I couldn't explain that one away because we both knew Buck well. That he wasn't a murderer.

"I'm sorry," I said softly, then reached out and stroked her cheek with my knuckles. Intentionally, I didn't answer her question. I couldn't. Not only because I didn't want to share anything about it with her, to protect her, but also because I had no answers. Yet.

She was so sweet, her skin smooth. I reveled in it. Got lost in her. I touched to soothe her, definitely, but to settle something in me as well. That I could now touch her freely. "I'm sorry I haven't been here for you. For your family. I was—am—hurting, too."

Saying those words was fucking hard.

The time I'd been back in Sparks was the longest I'd stayed anywhere since boot camp. That I was putting down roots, building a compound, a business, and a life here was new. And hard.

Sharing was hard after being trained to keep everything close.

"I know," she blurted, rushing to throw her arms around me.

Her forgiveness made my deceit even worse, but I soaked it up like a sponge. Wrapped my arms around her and held her against my chest in the embrace I should have offered at the memorial service and every day since.

"I'm going to make it up to you," I promised. I intended to make everything up to her—the lie I just told her. Letting her believe Buck was a fuck-up. Hurting her all those years ago. Ruining her sex life.

I intended to heal all the wounds I'd inflicted or spend my entire life trying.

Because Indigo Buchanan was mine.

Mine to protect. Mine to pleasure.

There was a knock on the door, and we stepped apart.

"That's probably Kennedy to get your house secure."

"A replacement lock is enough," she said.

I wasn't thrilled we'd spent the night with a busted front door, but while someone *had* broken in, this was Sparks, not behind enemy lines. I was used to waking up ready to kill, so I hadn't doubted Indi's safety. In fact, having my arms wrapped around her all night was the first time I knew she was truly protected. Broken door and all.

I just gave her a non-committal grunt in reply as I went to let Kennedy in. We'd get the lock replaced. Fix the door and jamb. Set up cameras. Motion relays inside. Sensors on the windows. Hell, even the fucking chimney. Whatever it took. We'd know everything that went on here from the command center.

Turned out, it wasn't only Kennedy waiting on the stoop, but Hayes, Taft, and even Gram.

Kennedy held a box. Hayes had one too. The two of them looked me over and grinned like Twee- dledee and fucking Tweedledum. Taft—the youngest of our team—stood beside Gram, a little more reserved. He'd missed the fun convo in the kitchen the day before about my issues with Indi.

"Gram. What are you doing here?" I asked the one sane person of the bunch.

My grandmother was eighty-one and sprier than Taft these days since he had an injured leg that had finished his military career with a medical discharge. Her hair was mostly salt with only a few strands of pepper. It was long and pulled back in the usual ponytail or bun. She had on a pair of overalls and a green t-shirt and old sneakers. A cloth sack was slung over a shoulder.

She wasn't one for show or flash or the use of too many words or prepared frozen meals. I loved that about her. Along with so many other things. I might have been a SEAL, but my Gram had more strength and resilience than I ever had. Hell, she could lead a class for BUDs.

"My car's fixed, and the boys brought me into town to pick it up," she replied. "Heard about the break-in and wanted to see for myself Indigo was all right."

Indi came around to stand in front of me. "Hi, Mrs. L. I'm fine. Come in out of the sun and have something to drink."

She elbowed me in the ribs to get me to move

and let the crew enter. The men stepped back for Gram to lead the way.

"Oh my." She glanced about. "What a mess."

We'd picked up. Some. But had been busy—with our clothes off.

There was still plenty for everyone to witness about the burglary.

"I've been meaning to do spring cleaning," Indi offered as she went to the kitchen and took glasses from the cabinet. Ones that hadn't been touched. Indi filled a glass of water at the sink and handed it off.

"Thank you, dear. Have you met my boys?" she asked.

Yup, Gram had taken my return, along with my intention to start a security company in her sewing room, in stride. After Kennedy showed up and we'd gotten Gramps' shop converted into a bunkhouse, she'd made extra lasagna for whoever arrived next. When we practiced demolitions in the back forty and built a pseudo obstacle course down by the creek, she'd wanted to try it out. The rope swing and even the C4.

"I'm Taft." The youngest of the team stepped forward to shake Indi's hand. At twenty-three, he'd had an entire career in the Navy ahead of him, but one sniper's bullet to his leg had ended it. When Lincoln had mentioned he was being discharged and needed a place to land, I'd bought him a one-way ticket to Montana. With physical therapy, he was able to have full use of his leg and could let us know when the barometric pressure was changing better than any weatherman.

"Hey," Indi replied, taking in his fair hair and the cowlick, making him look like nothing more than a sweet little kid.

"Hayes." The other guy said as he set the box he was carrying on top of the TV and gave Indi a wink. "We're going to wire this place up like Fort Knox."

Indi pasted on a blatantly fake smile. "I don't think that's necessary. Maybe just fix the door and a new lock. I can pick one up from my dad at the hardware store."

"That's—" I began, but Hayes cut me off.

"We know you can take care of yourself. Buck told us all about how you rock the wilderness," he told Indi. He lifted a packaged lock from the top and held it up. "Got this from your Daddy. He's all for us helping you get your house nice and safe. We men do this not because you are weak but because you're important."

Indi stared wide-eyed at Hayes, her mouth open.

"Okay," she finally muttered.

He nodded and offered her another wink.

Well, fuck me. No wonder he got the ladies. He knew exactly what to say. Instead of pushing, he'd greased that fucking wheel to get it to work.

Gram set her hand on Indi's arm. "Let the boys do their macho stuff while you walk me to get my car from Lee Landers. It's on the way to the sheriff's station. You need to sign a report, don't you?"

Hayes and Gram gave Indi a one-two punch, and I pinched my lips together to hide a smirk. I wasn't sure if they'd planned this in advance or if they should start doing standup.

"How did you know—" Indi asked Gram, but all my grandmother did was arch a brow in answer, which said it all. She knew everything that happened in town. "I'll... I'll get my bag," Indi murmured, completely trapped into letting us wire the shit out of her house. Even Gram was in on it.

Kennedy tucked a lollipop in his mouth, set his box on the kitchen counter, and started to pull stuff out. As Indi went into her bedroom, I strode over to Gram and kissed the top of her head. She smelled like Oil of Olay lotion, the same she'd used forever.

"Thank you," I murmured.

She reached up and patted my cheek. "You won't think it, but Buck would be pleased."

I tensed. "About what?"

"That she's finally yours."

I didn't respond. I didn't even breathe.

"I'm right, aren't I?" she prodded, looking up at me with the same blue eyes as mine.

I had to laugh and kiss her head again. "Gram, you're always right."

Indi came back, a cloth bag slung across her body. She'd braided her hair and put on shoes.

"We'll see you boys later," Gram called. She hooked her arm through Indi's and led her out of the house.

Indi glanced over her shoulder at me, and all I could do was smile and shrug.When they were halfway down the sidewalk, I spun around and took in my team.

"Where do you want us to start?" Hayes asked.

I went to Indi's desk and picked up the pile of papers I'd set there. "With this."They moved close, and I passed them to Taft.

"Indi had a bulletin board with all this tacked to it." I set my hands on my hips.

Taft flipped from one page to the next, scanning the articles and letters.

"This is all about Buck's death," he stated.

I nodded. "Need you to read it all and let me know any similarities," I told him.

Everyone underestimated the kid because he had farmboy looks. Before his knee was busted, he could swim faster and further than anyone on the team. But he wasn't just a babyface. He had an eidetic memory. Once he read or heard something, it was forever in the vault.

"A bulletin board?" Kennedy asked.

I nodded then tipped my head. "On her bedroom wall."

"Why?" Hayes asked, rubbing the back of his neck.

I met his dark gaze. "She's got the same questions as me. As all of us."

"She doesn't think her brother's a murderer," Kennedy stated.

I shook my head.

"Smart woman," Hayes added. "Although she'd be smarter if she hooked up with me instead of your sorry ass."

I bristled. "Watch it."

"You and Buck's sister?" Taft asked, glancing up from the papers for a second.

I wanted to say no. To say *hell no,* but that was wrong. It was a complete fucking lie. After Indi gave me her body, shared her desires, her needs, and trusted me to take care of them and see them all fulfilled, there was no going back.

"Yes. Me and Buck's sister. She's mine."

"She know that?" Kennedy asked, sliding the lollipop from cheek to cheek.

"Working on it." The last thing Indigo Buchanan was going to admit to was being mine if I told her that's what she was. It didn't matter that she creamed all over my dick or gave me her ass to spank, that woman needed to make a decision all on her own. In her own fucking time.

I, of course, liked to boss people around. It wasn't going to be easy.

Taft passed the papers to Kennedy and met my gaze. "She knows about the ranger team Buck was with. The guy Buck replaced——William Gentry. How Buck was killed. Even a later letter about how Buck was posthumously found guilty for murdering Abdul Tareen, the Afghan police officer."

"How'd she collect this intel?" Hayes asked.

Taft glanced around then pointed to her desk. "I'd say a simple Internet search."

"She doesn't believe Buck murdered Tareen."

"Did you tell her we're looking into it all?" Kennedy asked.

"Hell no," I replied. "I had to lie, to let her think it had to be dropped. I want her as far from this shit as possible."

"She's going to lose it when she finds out the truth."

"I think we're all going to lose our shit when we find out the truth. Because the person—or people— who are behind this aren't the patriots they're pretending to be. They've pinned it on Buck because dead men can't defend themselves. Whatever they're up to, it's still going on."

"Think William Gentry knew and was killed too?" Taft asked.

I nodded.

"Think all this was because she was poking around?" Hayes asked, taking in the mess strewn around them.

"From what Taft said, there's nothing new in what she's dug up. No mention of the translator's death which Lincoln shared with us the other day. This intel's stale. I'm not sure why they'd come after her, but I'm not taking any chances. Even if it was only fucking Goldilocks looking for porridge, I want this place secure."

They nodded at the order and got to work. Indi needed to be safe. Not because I owed it to Buck to protect her, but because Indi was mine, and I'd see nothing harm her.

CHAPTER
NINE

INDI

SINCE SPARKS WAS SO SMALL, Mrs. L and I only had to walk a few blocks to get to Landers Auto Shop. Buck had grown up with Lee, so I'd known him forever. He'd started working with his dad right after high school and had taken over the business a few years ago when his parents retired to Galveston, Texas, the beach and warm winters.

The short walk meant only a short amount of time for Mrs. L to ask me questions. She hid it under very skilled small talk, but I knew what was up. She'd learned about my latest guide trip, how my mother's huckleberry jelly making was going, whether or not my father would start selling snow shovels before Labor Day this year, and lastly, if I wanted to stay with her until I felt safe again.

"I have too many men at the house these days. It was good to see your laundry on the counter."

She eyed me pointedly as we made our way down the sidewalk under the warm sunshine. The clouds were caught on the peaks of the mountains and might make it into town for another afternoon shower.

I'd forgotten about the clothes I'd left behind. Ford had brought them by the day before, but they were on the living room floor with everything else. I did remember that my panties and bra had been on top of the small pile. A few days had passed, which meant they'd been sitting in Mrs. L's house. God, what had she thought?

That I'd been with Ford in her house? Taken them off... like, oh shit. Like when I was eighteen and done just that. She knew everything. *Everything.* She was sure to know about the naked rejection fiasco from nine years ago. And again a few days ago, then Ford staying the night before?

Yeah, she knew.

"I... I was caught in a rainstorm out hiking," I said weakly.

"Yes, that's what Ford said."

"It's not... Kennedy was there."

Mrs. L laughed and shifted her sack higher on her shoulder. "I heard about the green-house," she said, giving me an obvious reprieve. "I'm not sure why they've locked that place up tight when anyone can get in by breaking the glass."

"Exactly!" I tossed up my hands.

"Those boys want everyone to be safe. That's why Ford is staying with you now."

I opened and closed my mouth like a fish. The clues she had made it seem like Ford and I were a thing. After last night, I wasn't sure what we were. Lovers, as he'd said. But for how long? One night? Once my front door lock was fixed—although having four former SEALs in my house definitely meant more than a replaced deadbolt—life could get back to normal. But after having my ass spanked and fucked good and hard, I wasn't sure if I liked *normal.*

Still, Mrs. L didn't need to know all that.

"Oh, look, we're already here."

We'd made it to the small mechanic's shop. The only one in town.

"You can leave me here, sweetheart. Lee will take

care of me. Tell Dan I will sign his youngest's cast this week."

She gave me a wave and headed toward the open bay door where a car was lifted, and Lee was working beneath.

I continued down Main Street and turned south one block to the sheriff's station. The older building was one story, brick, and smelled like coffee. Not much happened in Sparks—besides my break in—so there was only a small staff. No one was manning the front desk, so I veered around it and went over to Megan. Her eyes were sharp and curious on my face as I approached.

Her chestnut hair was pulled back into a simple bun at the nape of her neck, and she wore a tan uniform, she was stunning. I felt like a frump next to her, but after knowing her forever, I couldn't hold it against her.

"So..." she said, the moment I walked up to her desk. "What's up with you and Ford?"

Unlike Mrs. L who more subtly worked information out of me, Megan was blunt. Maybe it was the law enforcement officer in her.

I wanted to lie, but it was impossible when my body was still sore in all the right places, my skin warm from his mouth and tongue.

Damn, I had been missing out.

Seriously missing out.

While I still wanted to blame Ford for my shitty sex life up until this point, some of my anger had shifted to Buck. A protective older brother was one thing, but he'd kept me and Ford apart. I could have had... *that*... as my first time.

That meaning the best sex known to womankind.

Sex with Ford had ruined me for all other men.

I couldn't help but wonder how different the trajectory of my sex life would have been had Ford slammed his bedroom door shut that night, locked out the world—and my brother—and fucked me thoroughly and completely my first time.

Oh well, I'd never know.

I still had a long way to go before I caught my stride in the sexual arena, but at least now, I knew how good it could be. How I could express myself, tell a man what I wanted and push past the fear of rejection. Because when Ford asked me what I wanted and I'd rolled onto my stomach... he hadn't pushed me away. He'd been into it. Into *me*.

"I don't know," I admitted finally. "We, um, are just getting reacquainted. We'd been avoiding each other since Buck's death."

The impishness left Megan's expression. "Yeah. Well, you've both been through a lot with that. It makes sense you'd avoid each other."

I doubted she knew Ford had been with Buck when he'd died, but everyone knew the rest. Everything I questioned and everything Ford and I had argued about when he'd seen my bulletin board. The board had accomplished nothing except making me more confused about my own brother and pissing Ford off. "Yeah."

"It also makes sense you might come together. A shared bond, you know?"

"Oh no," I said quickly, feeling my face grow warm. I knew how small-town gossip went. I didn't want Megan assuming Ford and I were *together-*together. Mrs. L certainly picked up on that. God, my bra had been sitting at her house for days! "I wouldn't go that far. I'd appreciate it if you didn't mention it to anyone else. You know how the gossip wheel works around here. Pretty soon the whole town will be asking for a wedding date."

Megan winced, and a stone sank to my gut.

"What?"

"Dan might have already told a half dozen people after we left your place yesterday."

"Oh God." I slapped my forehead. "He didn't."

Great, just what I needed—for Ford to find out I assumed I was his girlfriend or something. Like I needed to be rejected by him again. Ugh.

It wasn't just Ford who I didn't want to hear about this. There were my parents. And Brandon, who I'd been telling I was too devastated by Buck's death to consider dating anyone right now.

"Sorry. He came in carrying your underwear, Indi." She paused and gave me a pointed look. Because... yeah. Shit. "I doubt the guy would be delivering anyone else's to your house. Besides, you know there's not much else to entertain us around here." She sent me an apologetic smile.

I sighed. The perils of living in a small town.

"Well, I'm going to run to the Feed n' Seed to get coffees for the entire Navy SEALs team that descended on my house this morning to install security." I rolled my eyes.

Megan's back straightened. "Navy SEAL *team*? As in not just Ford? So more than one brawny, fit guy who might carry around my bra and panties? At your house right now?"

I smiled because *yeah*. Sparks was a small town which meant the dating pool for women our age was exceedingly small. I couldn't blame Megan for wanting to pull in a few more options. And none of the men were hard on the eyes. Or ovaries. "Would you care to help? I really could use another hand." I winked.

Megan was out of her chair and moving toward the door before I'd blinked. "I'll drive," she sang out. "Dan, I'll be back in a little bit. I'm going to get coffee at the Seed n' Feed. I'll have my radio on."

"We have coffee here," he called back.

"How many times do I have to tell you? Instant doesn't count!"

I laughed as I followed her out the door and into the sheriff's cruiser.

"I'd heard that Ford had some buddies up there," she said, putting her seat belt on. "How long are they here?" She started the engine and pulled out of the parking lot.

"They're living up there."

"They are?" She sounded as surprised as I'd been to find half of a SEAL team had taken up residence in Sparks without us knowing it.

"Yes. Ford has started a private security firm. Alpha Mountain Security."

Yeah, I'd looked it up.

"Hmm, that name is good. Ford's a total alpha male. And with that beard, mountain man."

I couldn't argue with her on that. "I don't think

he considers himself either of those two things. He and Buck were on Alpha Team in the SEALs, and well, you get the mountain part."

Megan offered a grunt in reply but probably liked her thinking better.

"He told me last night that there are people who pay a lot of good money for a team with their expertise."

She was quiet for a minute. I wasn't sure what part of hot SEALs living in Sparks and working security was the hottest. "Wow. Are we talking body-guard stuff? I wouldn't think there'd be much need for that in Montana."

"I believe the work is international," I said although I wasn't exactly sure. "But yes, bodyguard-ing, and I think more intense operations, as well. Ford told me he and a couple of the guys are leaving town next week on some job in South America."

"So, speaking of last night..." Megan paused dramatically, inviting me to dish.

I didn't bite as I stared out the side window. "Yes?" I asked with mock innocence.

"Sounds like you and Ford had a lot to talk about."

"Mmm, it wasn't all talking." I flashed a satisfied

smile at Megan, and her face broke into a matching grin.

"Okay! That's what I'm getting at." Her tone was congratulatory. "Who doesn't need an ex-Navy SEAL to, um, occupy their nights?"

I laughed as she pulled up and parked at the old Feed n' Seed, which Holly Martin had turned the grain office section of it into a coffee shop.

Oldtimer locals were gathered around the large wooden spools that served as tables and footstools as they reclined in Adirondack chairs, swapping tales.

Hopefully none of the tales involved me and Ford.

"Hey, Indigo, I heard your place got broken into," old Burt Hammond remarked as we climbed the steps to the wooden deck. "Megan, did you catch who did it, yet?"

"Not yet, Burt, but we're working on it," she called out with that sing-song quality of someone who has answered the same question at least a dozen times already. "But good news, the stop sign that got knocked down on Simpson is back up."

We stepped inside, and Holly came to the counter. "Morning, ladies. What's the news?"

This was how small town errands went. I could

never just enter a store and take care of business. There was an exchange that had to happen first, even with the young people, like Megan and Holly.

"Not much, just picking up some coffees to go," I said, trying to avoid turning the gossip wheel on the SEAL team.

"Heard your place got broken into. Is everything okay?" Holly was twenty-four and had used her business degree wisely. The Seed n' Feed held its own with ranchers and farmers in the area, but the coffee shop was a great addition.

"Yep, nothing of value was taken, just more an inconvenience than anything," I assured her. "May I have four coffees in to-go cups, please? Wait—make that five." I turned to Megan. "Did you want one?"

"Yes, please," Megan said. She leaned close and whispered, "I'm not dropping you off and missing the man candy show."

"Six then, but make two of those mochas," I said, remembering Kennedy liked hot chocolate as much as I did.

"Sure thing. Four regular coffees and two mochas to go." She moved efficiently behind the counter. "Where are you two headed?"

So much for not telling the whole story.

"There are some guys repairing the locks at my house and installing security," I said.

"Ford and his team?" Holly obviously knew more about Ford's new venture than I had. I ignored the stab of jealousy it produced because it was certainly possible the men had stopped in for coffee before.

I didn't have any rights to Ford. We'd only spent one night together.

Although we'd had sex multiple times.

"Uh, yeah."

Memories of just how incredible the sex had been flooded my brain, and I had to turn my head and look out the window to hide the heat I feared might be showing on my face.

"Have you met them?" I couldn't help but ask as she worked the machine that steamed milk.

"No, I heard from Mrs. L. She loves having the bunch of them up with her." Holly's smile was warm as she slid the first two coffees onto the counter.

"I'll bet she does—it must take the sting out of losing Mr. Ledger," Megan said, mentioning Ford's grandfather, who passed away a couple years ago.

"Here you go." Holly set the last drink on the counter that was the old grain office counter. "Do you need a drink carrier?"

"Yes, please." I offered her a smile and pulled out my wallet.

She produced one and loaded the coffees onto it. "Wouldn't mind if the team wanted to stop by here for their own coffee," she said with an impish smile.

So they hadn't been by to ogle the pretty and young Holly.

"Right? Why do you think I offered to drive Indi over there?" Megan laughed.

So long as they knew Ford was taken. My stomach somersaulted at the idea of him actually being mine. The man who'd occupied all my teenage fantasies actually fulfilling some of them.

But I was getting way ahead of myself.

One night.

I'd had one night with him. It probably meant nothing to him. This was a guy who'd likely had a new girl in every port. Who could have Megan or Holly. Hell, Megan *and* Holly.

I grabbed the drink carrier and Megan picked up the two remaining cups, and we headed to her patrol car.

"Be safe," Burt called as we passed him and his cronies.

"We sure will," Megan chirped in reply. Her radio on her utility belt chirped, but she silenced it.

A short drive later, we pulled up in front of my place.

"Damn," Megan said, eyeing Hayes' muscled body.

He was up on a ladder in front of my picture window, presumably installing a sensor or camera or some kind of electronic... thing. He could have been setting up a circus tent, and we wouldn't have known because—

"That ass," she breathed. "Can you imagine gripping that while..." She cut herself off then used her hand to fan her face.

"I know. That epic butt belongs to Hayes. They all look like that," I murmured as I pushed the door open and carried the drink tray out.

"Ladies." Hayes climbed down the ladder, his gaze laser-focused on Megan. I wasn't surprised he was staring. Megan was drop-dead gorgeous. Her mother had been a literal beauty queen—Miss Montana 1985, but she'd walked out on Megan's family when she was young. I suspected Megan became a sheriff to prove to herself and this town she was far different from her mom. That she would stick and was much more than a pretty face.

"I mean, Sheriff." Hayes had come up close and

took in Megan's uniform—or every inch of her body—and I would swear his voice had deepened.

"I'm not the sheriff," Megan said with a laugh.

"I'm Hayes." He stuck his hand out to shake hers. When he clasped it, he held it a really, really long time. They stared at each other as if tractor beams kept their gazes connected.

"Is that a first name or a last?" she asked.

Hayes flashed a dimpled grin. "It's my call sign."

"They all have presidents' names." I worked one of the coffees out of the tray and offered it to Hayes. "On account of Ford and Buck both sharing that honor." To Hayes, I said, "Coffee?"

"Yes, please." He picked up two cream packets from the pile on the center of the drink carrier.

"Why Hayes? I don't recall him doing anything noteworthy while in office," Megan commented.

"Ouch!" Hayes mimed pulling a knife out of his chest. "I'll have you know, Hayes was the first president to win by Electoral votes." He inched a little closer into Megan's personal space.

She didn't seem to mind.

"Wow. Impressive." I wasn't sure if she said that sarcastically, if she was actually impressed or if she hadn't been listening to what he said and had been hypnotized by his dark eyes.

"That's not why I picked it, though. It's because we haven't had a Hispanic president yet and Hayes has three of the five letters as my real last name. So there you go. That's how I picked it."

Megan narrowed her eyes and chewed on a lip like she was thinking hard.

"Reyes," Hayes filled in for her when she didn't offer a guess.

"Reyes," she repeated. "Nice to meet you, "Reyes-Hayes.""

"The pleasure is *all* mine." He winked as he took a sip of his coffee.

I could have been setting off fireworks, and they wouldn't have known because it seemed like they were shooting off their own just fine. *Okay.* I'd leave them to it.

I headed inside to find my place immaculate. Ford and friends had not only straightened up the mess, but it looked like they'd cleaned, too.

Kennedy had a laptop open at my kitchen table and was standing over it, tapping on keys, the customary lollipop tucked in his cheek.

"I brought you a mocha." I set it down beside him and was rewarded with his Hollywood-worthy grin.

"Caffeine. I could kiss you."

"Lips to yourself," Ford growled, walking in from my back door.

The sight of him took my breath away. I didn't know when I would stop being shocked by his new rugged appearance or its effect on my ovaries. Because military Ford had been hot, but this Montana man look was... more.

"Ford," I admonished.

"I mean it. Flirt with my girl, and I'll kick your ass."

My girl.

He called me his girl. Was this actually happening?

When his gaze landed on me and his mouth kicked up into a small smile, I swore I dropped an egg.

"You guys work quick." I sounded breathless as I pulled a coffee out of the container and offered it to him. He didn't take it, instead, encircling my wrist and pulling me close. His lips—not Kennedy's—met mine. And it wasn't a peck. No. His free hand cupped the back of my neck, and his tongue found mine.

There was no question he was staking his claim. I was glad he was doing it with a kiss instead of peeing a circle around me.

When he lifted his head, his blue eyes met mine

and held, as he finally took the coffee. "Yep, we're almost done here." He leaned closer, speaking for my ears only, his beard brushing over my skin. "Don't think this means I'm letting you sleep alone, though."

"We're done," Kennedy said. "Monitoring is up and running."

"Good," Ford replied. "Get out."

A hum started up between my legs, and my nipples stiffened at his command.

I couldn't tear my gaze away from Ford's. I heard Kennedy laugh, a laptop click shut. He called for Taft, and the front door closed.

"You're keeping up your bodyguard duties?" I murmured back.

He held my gaze and nodded. "That's right," he said. "*Permanently*."

Permanently? As in long term?

"You wet for me, Blue?" he asked.

I licked my lips then nodded.

"Get on your knees like a good girl and show me how much you want my dick."

I should smack him again. Or gasp and clutch my proverbial pearls in outrage. I didn't do either of those things. I did as he commanded, settling on the wood floor before him and opening up his jeans, so his dick bobbed free, an inch from my face.

I wanted him in my mouth. Needed it. Because when I licked the flared crown and a bead of pre-cum appeared, I felt powerful. I made him hard. Made him slap the to-go cup on the table and tangle his fingers in my hair. I did this to a SEAL, a huge mountain man.

Me, little Indigo Buchanan.

"Fuck. Indi," he hissed as I took as much of him as I could. "My little slut. Yes. Suck me down, but know, I'm coming in that pussy."

CHAPTER
TEN

FORD

YOGA PANTS WERE INVENTED by Satan. Not only did they make a man think of sin, but tortured him and his balls mercilessly as well. I let Indi lead the way up the mountain because she knew these hills like the streets of Sparks. At first, I'd smiled to myself, able to watch her taut ass as we went. But as the miles went on, it was becoming impossible not to bend her over a boulder, tug down that tight, form-fitting material and spank her ass for being such a tease.

It wasn't her fault. It was the devil and the inventors of spandex. Although her ass was perfect bare, too. I'd cupped and gripped it as we'd fucked the day before. And last night. And this morning.

So I knew that there was a small mole on her right cheek. I knew that muscular flesh jiggled when I spanked it. I knew what it looked like when my cock disappeared into her pussy when I took her from behind.

And now we were three miles from the trailhead on a perfect summer morning, and all my dick wanted to do was get inside her again. We'd decided to go on a hike because we needed to get out of her house. Away from her bed. Except it was pretty much impossible to keep my hands off her. To keep my dick from getting hard around her. Or thinking about her.

Now that she was mine, I was insatiable. And thank fuck, so was she.

She glanced at me over her shoulder and caught me staring. Again. She smirked.

"I'm only a man, Blue," I grumbled.

She stopped and spun about. Since the angle of the trail was steep, with her above me, we were eye to eye. For a rugged climb, she wasn't even breathing hard. We were far enough in on this harder trail that we'd left any tourists far behind.

"Sure, mountain man," she said, then cupped my

jaw, running her thumb over my beard. "Whatever you say."

I liked this side of Indi. Playful. Light. Open. It could be the sex. Yes, it was definitely the sex, but she was softer. Hell, she didn't hate me. If giving her as much dick as she wanted made that happen, I'd take one for the team.

"I like your beard," she admitted.

I cocked my head to the side and studied her. Took in the freckles across her nose. The soft arch of her brows. I'd never been able to study her this closely before. Because she hadn't been mine.

"Didn't want to stick with the short military look?" she asked.

She didn't know it, but oftentimes, the team had to let our hair grow out. Our beards too, as part of our missions. Except I'd let it grow in this time because I'd been kicked out and hadn't given a shit about rules and regs. I hadn't given a shit about much of anything except making things right. Now... I gave a shit about this woman.

I shrugged and played off all my feelings as nothing. "Too much work."

She laughed. "A buzz cut? Too much work?"

"I don't see a barber all that often now. Besides, the beard's warmer in the winter."

"You look... like a mountain man."

"So you said," I murmured, taking the time to stroke back her hair, sliding over the braid and taking hold of the ends and playing with the soft strands below the hair tie. I was mesmerized by the silky feel. The color.

"Why'd you leave?" she asked. A bird crowed nearby, and the wind whipped through the pines.

At first, I didn't know what she was talking about. She stayed quiet, and I lifted my gaze to meet hers. "Leave?"

"The Navy. You and Buck were in it for life. I mean, you planned to join up when you were what... ten?"

"Twelve," I said. It was the year after I moved in with my grandparents. "Gramps told me about his time in Vietnam. Same with your grandfather. I remember him."

"Pop Pop," she whispered and gave a small smile. "He always had candy in his shirt pocket."

"They told us stories. Of honor. Battle. Fighting for what was right," I explained, remembering those talks fondly. Buck and I had looked up to those men. "I wanted to make Gramps proud." I laughed, taking the time to think about it. "He gave me someone to look up to when my parents didn't."

"I think you made him proud whatever you ended up doing," she said. "Still. Why'd you leave?"

Because I'd gotten forced out. Because someone was corrupt and wanted me gone, so I didn't dig into bad shit. Because I was good enough to find out the truth which was supposed to stay hidden. The truth that had gotten Buck killed.

I couldn't say any of that to Indi. I wanted to tell her. Everything. Big sections of my time in the service were classified. I'd never be able to tell anyone.

But that had been regular SEAL mission shit. Normal secrets wives and family understood. If I told her the truth, she'd start to dig into Buck's service record. Get that bulletin board back in action again. Start digging.

This woman, with the sun glinting off her hair, the questioning, *trusting* look in her eye, was the one thing I had to take care of and protect. All the years of being a SEAL, all that training, was for her.

I couldn't blow it by telling her the truth. It was clear she didn't know it, or she wouldn't have asked. I'd keep her in the dark. Safe.

There was no other option.

"I... I couldn't keep going without Buck," I admitted. It was the truth. One hundred percent.

Except I'd also lied by omission. Because she thought I meant emotionally. I meant literally. The Navy wouldn't allow me to stay in with Buck dead. Period.

The words were bitter on my tongue. I was fucked no matter what I did. But I'd do anything, *anything,* to protect her.

"I miss him," she admitted. Her eyes welled with tears.

"Yeah, Blue. I do too." Fuck, did I. Knowing he was dead and some bastard had not only killed him but ruined his name and honor?

"He'd hate us for moping over him," I said.

She laughed and sniffled. "He'd hate that we're together."

I wrapped my arms around her, set my palms beneath her water backpack then lower still to cup her spandex-covered ass. "He'd hate it at first, but it's not about him any longer."

She didn't say anything else, only nodded, then turned and started up the trail again.

"You wear leggings like that when you're on a guide trip?" I asked after a few minutes.

"I usually have on regular pants. With pockets. I have to carry stuff for more than just me."

"Like what?"

"I might not be an Eagle Scout or a SEAL, but I can hold my own in the wilderness."

I didn't doubt her, that she believed that, but she was a little slip of a woman, and the wilderness was unforgiving.

"Tell me."

I needed to be distracted.

"Well... a mega-first aid kit. GPS. Health bars for emergency fuel. Multipurpose tool. That kind of stuff. What do you take on your jobs as a security consultant?"

"Same things, plus a few more."

"A few more things, like SEAL stuff?"

I nodded. Like K-Bar knives, semi-automatic pistols, and rifles. Sometimes explosives and other things that go boom.

"When we leave tomorrow, we'll be safe, Blue. We're trained for everything." I'd told her about our latest job, that Taft would be around. It was a shit time to leave her, but I had no choice. This trip was time-critical.

"So am I," she countered.

"I have a team though. You always lead a group solo?"

She shrugged. "Not always. Sometimes one of the other guides joins me. Sometimes Brandon."

I frowned at that guy's name. "What's your deal with him?"

She didn't slow her steps as she made her way up the rugged trail, but she was quiet for longer than expected.

"He's been my boss for a few years."

"And?"

"And a mistake."

Some small animal scurried under nearby brush as we passed.

A mistake.

That meant... no. It wasn't fair to want to turn back down the mountain, go into the guide office and rip the guy's head off. If *mistake* meant a past lover, then he'd treated her wrong since she'd admitted she'd never come with a man before.

Meaning Brandon hadn't seen to her needs.

"A SEALs specialty is wet work."

She tripped over a rock and stumbled, easily righting herself. She turned to stare at me, wide-eyed. "Wet work?"

I crossed my arms over my chest and waited. "My team can make him disappear. Quickly or painfully."

"Oh my God, seriously?" When I didn't reply and just stared, she continued, "Possessive, much?"

"You have no idea, Blue." Now that I knew what

her pussy felt like milking my dick as she came, I sure as shit was possessive. No one else would hear her cries of pleasure. See her gorgeous body flush with arousal. Know her taste. Her scent.

Her mouth fell open then a grin spread across her face. "Then am I able to claw the eyes out of all the women you've fucked? I mean, fair's fair."

"Then Brandon's a dead man?"

She huffed and shook her head. "I want to take over his business but not that way."

"Why the hell would you want to buy that loser out?"

"How do you know he's a loser?" she countered.

I raised a brow and gave her a look that screamed *seriously?* "Any man who can't satisfy a woman is a loser."

She pursed her lips and considered. "Probably true."

"Probably? So why do you want to buy him out? Start your own company."

She toed the dirt and watched as the pebble she kicked skittered down the hillside. "I need the equipment, and it would be cheaper to buy it from him than get it all new. Besides, I'm just a guide. I don't have the business side of it down. Sparks Outdoor Adventures has clients and connections."

I moved close to her. "Baby, you've got connections. An entire town to support you."

"People of Sparks don't need me to take them into the woods."

I cocked my head and studied her. I hadn't seen her this way other than when she talked about her skills in the sack. She was unsure of herself. I didn't like that.

"What would you do if something went wrong on a trip?" I asked.

Her blue gaze lifted to mine. "Call it in. Triage. Assess the weather. Decide if hiking out is best or hunkering down for rescue."

"If it's hiking out?"

"Follow the trail back. Or find water and follow it downstream." She tipped her chin a little higher. "My brother was the SEAL, but I can survive in the wild, Ford."

I tipped her chin up. "I know. That doesn't mean I want you to."

"We hiking or talking?" she countered.

"Or I can tug down those leggings and get in you again."

A slow smile spread over her face. "Only if you catch me."

She turned and sprinted up the trail. I watched

her get a head start. Laughed. Fuck, she was incredible. And if she thought she'd ever be able to get away from me, she was fucking mistaken.

I took off after her. Enjoying the chase. As easily as I ate up the distance between us, I realized I'd been chasing her for years. Searching the world for someone to fill Indi's spot, but I'd never found her. Because she'd always been right here. In Sparks.

Waiting.

I snagged her around the waist and lifted her off her feet. She laughed, and it caught on the breeze. I couldn't help but smile. Her backpack was wedged between us, but I didn't put her down. I carried her off the trail, past a large ponderosa pine and fuck, yes. To a large boulder in the bright sunshine. I set her on her feet for a moment to spin her about, then hoisted her up to sit on the large rock. Glancing back the way we came, I couldn't see the trail, which meant if there was a hiker coming by, they wouldn't see us either.

Indi parted her knees, and I stepped between, pushed the straps of her backpack off her shoulders and set it on the rock beside her. Then I hooked a hand behind her neck and kissed her. It had only been a few hours since I'd been inside her, but that was too long. I kissed her fiercely. Almost roughly in my need for her.

"I'm not getting naked Ford," she said when I pulled back. Her blue eyes were hazy and her breathing ragged.

"Don't need to do that for what I have in mind."

Her eyes widened slightly, and her gaze dropped to my lips.

"Lean back."

Slowly, she settled her elbows behind her, allowing me to snag my fingers into the waistband of her leggings and work them down. She lifted her hips to help, and I tugged her little thong with the stretchy fabric, so it settled around her lower thighs.

Grabbing her ankle, I pushed her legs up and back, so her knees were against her chest and her pussy was tipped up. Fuck, I couldn't miss how wet she was on those pretty pink folds. With one hand on her thigh keeping her in place, I ducked my head and licked up her slit.

"Ford!" she cried.

"Shh, Blue. Those sounds are just for me."

No one was around, but I wasn't going to risk anyone overhearing us.

She was calling *my* name when I ate her out.

I cupped her, spread her honey all over her pussy, then slipped two fingers into her.

"This is going to be fast. You're going to come for me, then I'm going to flip you over and fuck you good and hard, Blue."

"Yes," she hissed as I curled my fingers over her g-spot and sucked on her clit.

It didn't take long. It seemed Indi was primed to come when I got my mouth on her or my dick in her. Her moan was low and deep and stifled by the arm she'd flung over her face.

I felt her clench around my fingers, and her wetness dripped all over my beard.

I loved knowing I'd have her scent on me all day.

I stood, set her hiking boots on one shoulder and opened up my jeans, and worked my boxers down enough so my dick sprang free. I quickly sheathed it in a condom I pulled from my back pocket—Indi wasn't the only prepared one on this outing—and slid home.

I held myself still as I crammed her full.

So hot. So wet. Her pussy clenched. Someone could put a gun to my head, and I wouldn't be able to stop fucking her.

I pulled back, thrust deep. Indi's fingers clawed

at the rock. Realizing the unforgiving surface might hurt her back, I cupped her ass and lifted her up.

"Hurry, Ford," she breathed.

She was fully clothed except for her lowered pants, but I couldn't miss watching the way my dick disappeared inside her. With her legs trapped together, she was so fucking tight.

Shit. I wasn't going to last.

"Touch yourself. Show me how you'll come when I'm away."

She reached between her thighs and circled her clit with two fingers.

"Good girl. Fuck, Blue. Such a good girl."

I fucked into her as she rippled and came. My balls tightened, and nothing was keeping me from letting go. I saw stars. Went blind. Felt tingles down my spine. The best fuck ever.

Me, Indi, out in the wild. Wild ourselves.

CHAPTER ELEVEN

FORD

"I WANT ALL the equipment checked and packed for the op this weekend," I told Hayes.

We were in the war room—formerly Gram's sewing room, which served as our temporary command center.

We met every morning at 0800 hours. One thing I'd learned in the military was regimen, and—except for my mountain man beard—I hadn't dropped it when I came home. My mood may have been dark as hell, but at least I had a goddamn routine.

And a lot of wood to chop.

It was funny how different it all felt today, though.

I had Indi in my life. Everything had changed. Clearing Buck's name was even more important because I didn't want her to suffer another day without knowing the truth.

I also hated keeping this effort from her, but it was for her own protection.

"Already done, Master Chief."

I heard the flap of the dog door, then Roscoe's nails clicking across the wood floor. He trotted up to me and nudged my thigh with his nose. I reached down and scratched his ear. "Good. Kennedy, are the flights all set?"

"Yes. The commercial flight out of Billings at 0615 hours and a private one to Santiago from Houston at 1300 hours."

Roscoe abandoned me and made his way around the room, getting pets from everyone.

We were headed to Chile as protection for a diplomat. Another had been kidnapped by guerillas and taken to... potentially north into the mountains of Peru. We'd split up, offering bodyguard and protection services as well as extraction. If we found the woman quickly, we'd be home within the week.

My cell rang in my pocket, and I pulled it from

my shirt. The sight of Indi's name on the screen had me smiling. "Hey, Blue."

"Hey yourself. I got a call from Megan. Turns out, the break in? It was the Mellmans' son, Roger."

I frowned, trying to picture the kid. "He has an older brother?" I asked, running a hand over the back of my neck.

"Yes. Roger's nineteen. Had mental health and drug issues. Been living in his parents' basement since he was kicked out of MSU. He was caught on the Zinther's doorbell cam breaking into the house across the street. He was caught three doors down by Mrs. Ellerby and her shotgun. Looks like he hit a string of places looking for drug money."

I sighed in relief. I wasn't thrilled a kid was doing shit like this, but at least the hunt was cash not hurting anyone but himself.

"He's been sent to rehab in Idaho."

"Good to know," I said.

"Thought you'd want to hear about it."

"Thanks. I'll be by later."

"You don't have to," she countered. "I know you're leaving super early tomorrow."

As if I'd skip even a few hours in Indi's bed with her in my arms. Naked.

"I'll be by later," I repeated.

She laughed. "All right, mountain man."

She hung up, and I realized everyone was eyeing me. Even Roscoe although his attention span was short because he went to his dog bed in the corner, circled three times, then flopped down with a sigh.

"They caught the kid who broke into her place." I gave a rundown of what Indi had shared.

He was in rehab and hopefully on the right track. Indi was safe, and the house as secure as Fort Knox.

"I feel better about leaving now," I admitted.

"You sure you don't need me to come along, Master Chief?" Taft asked.

I knew the guy still felt sidelined, but his knee recovery had been slow. Hell, the doctors said it was a miracle they saved his lower leg at all. He'd had seventeen surgeries on it and a missed infection raging for months that was finally beginning to heal.

"I need you for protection here. Even if the Mellman kid did the breaking and entering, I'd feel better knowing one of us is around. If I could get her to stay here with Gram, I would."

"But your woman's got you by the balls," Kennedy added.

I glared. "You lock that house down tight?"

His grin slipped away. "You questioning my skills?"

"You questioning my balls?"

"I'm on it, Master Chief." Taft straightened his already stiff spine as he replied. I'd been stripped of my rank, but Taft had yet to call me Ford. Not once in all the time he'd been here. "Want me to stay at her place?"

Kennedy and Hayes both snickered at the same moment I exploded, "No!"

I glared at all three of them. Taft was almost a decade younger. Cute in that corn-fed farm boy sort of way. No way was he staying anywhere near Indi where she could come out of her bathroom in only a towel.

Fuck no.

"Of course you're not going to fucking spend the night with her," I raged, the idea of any guy sleeping in that small house besides me turning me irrationally jealous and possessive.

Taft held his hands up in surrender. He honestly hadn't been fucking with me—the kid was too earnest. Kennedy and Hayes apparently thought my reaction was hilarious, though, because they couldn't stop sending each other looks and grinning.

"You can sleep outside her place in a vehicle."

"I don't know if that's really necessary," Gram said from the doorway, her voice making Roscoe perk up and thump his tail on his bed. She had a crossword puzzle book and pen in her hands. She had no problem eavesdropping on our war talk. I probably shouldn't let her hear anything for her own safety, but I couldn't bring myself to leave her out. She was sharp as a tack and sometimes had good insight to offer.

This wasn't one of those moments.

"Taft can monitor everything from here. I have security at her place as tight as a nun's—" Kennedy cut himself off and cleared his throat.

Gram gave him a pointed look, but the corner of her mouth twitched.

I growled but agreed. I was probably going overboard, and maybe Indi did have my balls around her neck like a Wilma Flintstone necklace, but I didn't give a shit. "Fine. But you don't sleep. I want you monitoring that shit all night long."

Kennedy and Hayes made soft rumblings under their breath but shut up when I glared their way. Again.

"Did you dig anything else up around Gentry's death?" I was in one of the dining room chairs we'd pulled in. Hayes was in the rocking chair, Kennedy at the desk slash sewing machine table. Taft had been in Gram's tufted armchair but stood for her to take the spot.

"Yep." Kennedy reached for the candy bowl on the desk and rooted through it to pull out a caramel square, which he unwrapped. He was pausing for dramatic effect, and I wanted to punch his nose in. "Talked to Lincoln. Told me his record lists him dishonorably discharged for a failed drug test, just like you, which means no death bennies—just like Buck."

Gram huffed.

Buck's death benefits had been withheld because of the drug and murder charges against him.

"Sounds to me like you boys just need to bark further up that chain of command. That Ranger team is clearly the link," Gram said, setting her crossword book in her lap.

I nodded in agreement with Gram then looked to Kennedy. "See if Lincoln can find out any hint of current drug trafficking in the area where he was killed."

"Will do. That it?" Kennedy asked, tossing the caramel in his mouth.

I nodded.

"What do you want me to do, Master Chief?" Taft asked.

"Gram, you need Taft to work on any projects?" I asked.

"No, I think you boys have put everything in tip-top shape around here already," she said. "The construction crew knows what to do on your house build."

"Find a way to make yourself useful," I grumbled at Taft.

"Yeah, there might be some wood that needs chopping," Hayes said with mock innocence.

"Oh yeah, we definitely don't have enough logs split around here," Kennedy said.

Yeah, I might have chopped at least three years' worth already. "Fuck off, both of you."

"Fucking off." Kennedy saluted with an unwrapped lollipop he'd picked up out of the bowl. I had to wonder how many cavities he had.

"Fucking off," Taft muttered with a grin.

"Already fucked off," Hayes said, leaving the room.

Gram smiled indulgently, our colorful language not affecting her in the slightest. She stood and moved into Kennedy's vacant seat, right beside me. "You're getting closer to clearing Buck's name," she observed.

I stabbed my fingers through my hair. I just connected with Indi, and I was off on a job on another continent. Then there was the ever-present need to solve Buck's shit. My own, too.

It was piling up, the need for a woman, the frustration with the government that I thought had my back.

"Not close enough."

She set her aged hand on top of mine. "No, this latest death—poor man—is going to unearth some things. It's too big a coincidence to have two translators from the same team dead. This will have to get the attention of military police."

I liked her optimism, but if they could pin so much on Buck and kick me out, whoever was leading this clusterfuck was smart enough to make Gentry's death look like a suicide, so it wouldn't be noticed.

"Not sure that's what we want, Gram," I said. There was no connection between Indi and anything that happened in Afghanistan, but her safety still scared the shit out of me. I couldn't protect Buck. I couldn't let her down in the same way, even though we were in Sparks. Far from a war that was now over.

"Of course, it is. Not everyone is corrupt in the

military. You will ultimately need someone on the inside to help you pull this case together."

"We have Lincoln." Our old CO needed us as much as we needed him. His hands were tied with protocol and regulations. My team had none.

"Yes, of course, but he's not working on this case in an official capacity. You need military police on it."

"Perhaps. Maybe I'll reach out to the family of the other translator. See what they were told."

She nodded. "That's a good idea. Have you shared all this with Indi?"

"No," I barked too sharply. "I need her to stay out of it."

She frowned, the wrinkles on her face deepening. "Why?"

Why? "People are dying over this. I got dismissed. I can't have Indi stirring the pot somehow and getting the attention of the wrong people."

"By sharing your burdens with her?"

"Exactly."

Gram nodded thoughtfully. "How long do you think you can hide it from her?"

"Until it's solved." I stood from the table and paced around the small room.

"But you're planning on...continuing your relationship with her."

"Yes."

"May I ask a question, Ford?"

"Shoot."

"Are you getting into a relationship with Indi out of your guilt and sense of responsibility for Buck's death?"

"Hell, no!" I exploded then dialed it back because, after all—it was Gram. "Sorry. No. Not at all."

Of course, Gram didn't know about the bedroom incident years ago or that Indi and I had shared an attraction for much longer than the few days we'd been together now.

"I always wanted Indi." It was the first time I'd actually voiced that truth. "I just couldn't pursue her before. Buck would've killed me."

I could see now—all along it had been about Buck. His demands that I stay away from Indi. The bro code. What he'd wanted. I'd honored that for almost ten years. But why? Why had he wanted me to stay away? Because he didn't think I was good enough for his sister? I'd had his back in fucking battle. I'd held him when he'd died. I was the one who was going to clear his name. Maybe he thought no one was good enough for her. It didn't matter. Indi had to make her own choice. And so far, for some fucking reason, she'd chosen me.

"Ah," Gram said knowingly. "That may have been true at one time. But you know it's not anymore. If Buck was alive, he'd be thrilled to know two of the people closest to him were in love."

In love.

I stood and paced the small room, the braided rag rug beneath my feet.

Was I in love with Indi?

Definitely.

This... thing with her went beyond a physical attraction. Indi was everything I admired in a woman. She was smart and funny and damn capable. She and I had shared values and a shared history that involved both our love and our grief over Buck. It included growing up in the same small town. She'd been around through thick and thin, from the day I moved to Sparks, as much a part of my adolescence as Buck had.

"Buck caught us together once when we were on leave," I admitted, staring into the kitchen. "It didn't go well."

"Well, that's different," she admitted. "A sailor on leave is trouble. Of course, he wouldn't want that for

Indi, even with you. Because that's what it would have been."

"True," I agreed.

"Ford."

I turned and met her gaze.

"Regardless of why you returned, you're here now. Staying in Sparks. Putting down roots. With your team. You're definitely worthy of her. Buck would be overjoyed. So would your grandfather."

Gram's words eased some of the tension I'd carried since I'd claimed Indi. I wanted to believe them. "I don't know about *overjoyed*..."

"Yes, overjoyed," Gram insisted, nodding for good measure. "Their parents, too. It's about time you got over there to visit with them again, don't you think?"

So it hadn't gone unnoticed that I'd avoided Mr. and Mrs. Buchanan. But it *hurt* to think about seeing them. Still...

I rubbed my beard. "Yeah."

I'd been meaning to for a long time, except I kept finding reasons to put it off. But Gram was right. I was dating their daughter—no, not dating. That didn't sound right. It was so much more than dating. We didn't need to *date*. I knew everything about her. All that was important. Indi was mine. I didn't know if she knew it yet, whether she suspected that I was completely all-in with her—even though I had told her I wanted forever—but she'd figure it out soon enough.

Now that I had her, nothing would ever make me let her go.

CHAPTER
TWELVE

INDI

FORD HAD BEEN GONE for three days. In that time, I'd cleaned my house from top to bottom. Roger Mellman had done me a weird favor, pointing out stuff I didn't need or forgot I even had. I hadn't lived in the house long, and I still filled a few boxes for the Lutheran church's donation bin. Taft had stopped by mid-clean out and helped me. By helped, I meant he carried, and I watched. I'd had dinner with my parents one night, played cards with Taft and Mrs. L another, and kept myself busy.

I never realized how alone I'd been until Ford and I got together. I'd been going about my life just fine hating the guy and then... wham. He kissed me, and everything changed. He'd said forever, and he didn't lie, but that length of time was a big commitment. I wasn't holding him to it although I had a feeling my heart wouldn't do so well if things went wrong.

I was still raw and hurt from Buck's death. Nothing could take away that ache or emptiness, but Ford had made me feel. I'd been numb for so long that I felt different. Felt alive.

"Earth to Indi."

I blinked and spun around in the storeroom.

"Brandon." I set the life preserver I was holding on the table where I was collecting items for the upcoming guide trip. I was to be gone for a week and needed to pull together items for rafting as well as camping to either give to the guests or pack up in the rafts.

"You were staring at the wall. Are you okay? Need a hug?"

I frowned. "Um... no. I don't need a hug. I'm pulling supplies together for the trip."

"You've been in here a while."

I sighed. "Lots of things to organize. Deke's coming in to confirm everything."

Deke Jacks was another guide. Since we would

be out with six in the group, and we'd need two rafts, he was the other guide on the trip.

"About that. We're going to trade it up. Deke and Jasper will take the rafting crew, and you can take Jasper's hiking group over the pass and to Glacier Lake."

I frowned. "Why the switch?"

"Three more signed on for the rafting trip. Between the supplies and the rafts, it'll be too heavy for you."

"It's never been an issue before," I replied, bristling.

He scratched the back of his neck, his hair sliding over his shoulder. His appearance was more of a wasted skateboarder than a guide shop owner.

"This new trip is shorter, and... I need you around here."

"Why?"

He shrugged his t-shirt-clad shoulder. "I've got tickets to that bluegrass festival next weekend."

Anger welled thick and bubbly like lava. "You switched trips on me because you want me to go to a music festival?" I pushed past him and out of the storeroom. "Unbelievable." I flipped off the light on the way out, leaving him in darkness.

"I know you like that kind of music."

The guide office was a cross between a small wilderness store and a travel agency. There was outdoor gear for sale if a guest forgot to pack something and desks with computers to plan and organize all aspects of adventure travel.

I turned away from the entrance and faced Brandon. I heard him follow because he dragged his feet like a lazyass. "I *told* you I'm not interested."

"You were over the winter."

"Once."

"Are you turning me down because of Ford Ledger?"

"What?"

He shrugged again, and I looked at him with new eyes. Ford was right, Brandon was a loser. He couldn't grasp that when I said I wasn't interested, I *really* wasn't interested. That there had to be a reason, like another guy, why I wouldn't hop back in bed with him.

"Heard he's at your house every night."

Heard? Or maybe he drove by and saw Ford's old truck in my driveway.

"He is." I wasn't going to deny it. My parents knew. So did Mrs. L. I was twenty-seven, not eighteen, and I had no reason to sneak around. I also wasn't going to give him any other details. It was none of his business.

"Did you think about what I offered, that I'd buy your business from you?" I asked, switching topics.

He laughed. "Yeah, I thought about it. The idea's good, so I asked around. Got a good deal from a guy in Missoula."

My mouth fell open, and my stomach clenched up tight. "You talked to a guy in Missoula? You didn't even wait to see what I'd offer. It could be more money." *You idiot,* I wanted to add, but that wasn't going to help anything.

He shrugged... again. God, he was annoying! "Fine. Give me your figure, and I'll consider."

I spun on my heel and went out the front door. The summer sun was high in the sky, and I took a breath of the fresh air. Felt the pull to escape into the mountains, away from dicks like Brandon. Away from the emptiness of losing Buck. Of seeing my parents broken over his loss. Of... everything.

"You okay?"

I turned. Taft was walking my way down the sidewalk. He wore running shorts and a plain white t-shirt. Sweat made his blond hair damp and his body... glisten. "Did you *run* here from the Ledger place?"

He lifted the hem of his shirt to wipe his face. I didn't even know a twelve-pack was possible other than in romance novels.

"It's only five miles."

Ford had told me about his injury, but other than the jagged scar on the outside of his left knee, I wouldn't have known he'd been hurt.

"Right. You'll run back, too, of course. I mean, it'll only be ten miles total. You single, Taft?"

His pale brows winged up. "I like my balls intact, Indi."

I frowned then realized what he meant. "Not me. I mean, you're... hot and all." Understatement of the year. "But I'll stick with Ford. I meant the other ladies in Sparks."

He shrugged. "While the others are gone, the only women I'm looking at these days are you and Gram."

I shook my head. "Fine, fine. I don't have to be a baby SEAL to know evasive techniques."

He grinned, then his smile slipped. A head tip toward the guide shop came before he said, "Need me to kill him for you? It'd be fun."

"What is it with you guys wanting to kill people?"

"We don't do it all that often anymore. These

days we specialize in assholes who fuck with women."

For some reason, it felt oddly reassuring to know I had a whole team of overprotective men watching out for me.

"That's oddly sweet of you, but killing Brandon's not necessary."

He took a step closer. "Scaring the shit out of him would be fun too. Haven't done any late-night infiltration and interrogation in a while."

I couldn't help but laugh. "I'll keep that in mind."

If Taft or any of the other guys messed with Brandon in my defense, there was no way he was going to sell to me. And if he did, I didn't want him to do it because they'd put his balls in a vise or threatened to remove his fingernails with pliers.

I should just quit and never come back. Walk down the sidewalk and keep on going. But I had a mortgage to pay. Bills. Then I thought of Ford, of what he'd said.

That I could open my own place. I practically ran the business for Brandon, no matter what he thought. I'd still need to buy equipment, but that might be easier than dealing with Brandon. For now, I wasn't going back in the shop. Ford had offered to make Brandon disappear. If he were in town, I might actually take him up on it.

That meant I needed a break. To work off this anger. Unfortunately, the best way I knew to do that was with Ford and his talented dick.

CHAPTER
THIRTEEN

FORD

IT WAS two in the morning, and Indi was tucked into bed. Asleep. I stood outside her house, noting the lights were off. The neighborhood was quiet. I should leave her be, come by in the morning, but I couldn't.

We'd been gone a week, and I couldn't wait a second longer to be with her. To be *in* her.

I pulled out my cell and sent her a text that I was outside and coming in. As far as I knew, she didn't have a gun, but the last thing I wanted to do was scare the shit out of her. Especially after the break-in.

I palmed the key Kennedy had given me and slid it into the new lock. It opened easily. There were no beeps on the security system—a quick indication for burglars that there was an alarm—and typed in the code. No doubt Kennedy had just received an alert about the door opening, which he knew was me from the cameras outside.

Only the light over the kitchen stove was on, but I knew the second Indi came out of the bedroom. Her white tank top glowed in the moonlight through her front window. I'd have to talk with her about getting blinds.

"Hey, Blue."

She stood there for a second, a mere moment before she ran at me and launched herself in my arms. My hand went to her ass as she wrapped her legs around my waist. Her mouth on mine.

Fuck, *this.*

She was sweet and warm and soft. Everything I wasn't. She was a physical reminder that there was good in this world. That there were things untainted.

"I missed you," she breathed against my lips.

I spun, pressing her into the front door and rolled my hips, so she felt how hard I was. I could feel the heat of her center through her tiny sleep shorts and my pants.

My dick had never been harder. My balls ached to fill her. To sink into her.

"This is going to be fast," I said, kissing and nipping down the line of her neck.

"Yes," she breathed, her fingers scrambling to tug up the hem of my shirt. I pulled back enough to reach behind my head and pull it off.

"Yes," she said again, running her palms over my chest.

"Take me out," I growled.

I was driven now by a need to fuck. To mate. To claim. The job had been successful, but not before we'd been forced into a gun battle to extract the diplomat.

Using my hips, I held her braced against the door, one hand cupping her ass, the other pressed into the wood by her head.

Her ragged breathing made her tits heave, and I had to see them. As she worked my zipper down, I pulled up her tank, so it bunched under her arms. Those lush swells bare to me. Cupping one, I kneaded the soft flesh, plucked at the nipple.

"Fuck," I hissed when she pulled me free and gripped me at the base and stroked me from root to tip.

I all but slapped her hand away, took myself in

hand and used the weeping tip to nudge her sleep shorts to the side. Easily finding her dripping center, I notched at her entrance and drove deep.

Her back arched, and we cried out together.

Fuck. This. Here. I could get lost in this woman. "This was all I thought about," I admitted, showing she was my biggest weakness, my ultimate distraction.

Her heels dug into my ass, pulling me in. "Please," she begged.

I wasn't the only one desperate.

I pulled back, rammed home. She was snug and perfect.

"Like that?" I murmured.

"Harder."

She tried to move, but I had her pinned, her nails dug into my biceps as I lost myself in her. There was no rhythm, not finesse. Just chasing pleasure. Giving it.

"I need you to come, Blue," I growled.

I wasn't leaving her behind.

Her head tipped back. "I... I can't."

My hand slid down the door and cupped her breast. My fingers brushed the base of the necklace about her neck. I pinched her nipple, and her eyes flew open. Met mine.

"You can. You will."

She shook her head. "I'm not—"

I shifted my grip on her ass, so my fingers slipped between those taut cheeks. My middle finger brushed against my dick as I pummeled into her to coat it in her cream then pressed against her back entrance.

"Ford!"

Yeah, that worked. Her pussy clenched me like a fucking fist.

Carefully, I pressed my finger into that virgin ass up to the knuckle.

"Oh God."

I leaned in, sucked at her neck. "That's my dirty girl. You'll come now that I'm in that tight ass. Think what it'll feel like when it's not my finger but my dick. You'll be ass up, pussy dripping. Begging me to take you."

"Ford," she whimpered. She just got wetter, soaking my dick.

"Come," I commanded.

This time, she did. Her body clenched then released a scream tearing through the quiet house.

I might have gone through BUDs training and never gave in, but I couldn't survive another second of Indi's pussy. My knees buckled. My balls drew up, and I spurted into her. Thick, hot pulses of cum that went on and on.

My hand slapped against the door, my fingers clenched her ass, my finger in her back hole remaining deep.

I couldn't catch my breath, panting against her sweaty skin.

"I'm not done with you. Not even close."

Once I had strength back in my legs, I pushed off the door and carried her into her bedroom. Dropped her on the bed and crawled over her.

Yeah, I wasn't done. I didn't think I ever would be.

———

INDI

HE WAS HERE. Hovering over me. His gaze roved over me. My tank was bunched beneath my armpits, and Ford's pants were pushed down low on his hips. That was as far as we'd gotten in taking our clothes off. I was sweaty and sticky and... God, I had his cum slipping from me.

"Um... Ford," I murmured. My pussy ached from

the hard pounding—not that I was complaining, and like he'd said, we weren't done.

Still...

"Yeah?" he asked, tucking his fingers into my sleep shorts and sliding them down.

"We didn't um, use anything."

He'd shifted, so he stood at the foot of the bed, my shorts dangling from his fingers. His gaze wasn't on me but between my thighs. He dropped the fabric to the floor and slid his calloused palm up the inside of my leg then pushed my knee wide.

I was open and exposed, and he ran a thumb over my pussy.

"I mean, I'm on the pill and all that but—"

"I'm clean," he said on a growl. "Fuck, this has to be the sexiest thing I've ever seen. My cum slipping from you."

His dick jutted toward me, thick and long. It was shiny, wet from being inside me. He hadn't taken off a bit of clothing.

"You're okay forgoing condoms?" I asked. "I mean, it wouldn't be like when I was eighteen. I'm not trying to trap you."

His head snapped up, and his eyes narrowed. Like a predator, he slowly crawled over me, so his face was right above mine. I couldn't see anything but him.

"Let's get some things straight right now. Maybe it's because I've been gone a week, or maybe that beautiful brain of yours is still a little fucked up over that night."

I swallowed. He was so intense, but his voice was low and almost gentle. Still, I felt him coiled tightly, as if he were about to snap. His intensity was powerful. Potent.

"I'd never put you at risk. Not for an STD or pregnancy. I saw your pills in the bathroom. I admit, we could have talked about ditching the condoms, but I couldn't wait another second to get inside you. But don't you ever, *ever,* think I'm walking out on you. I'm here. With you. For good. Got me?"

I nodded, my hair sliding across my blanket.

His gaze roved over my face. "I don't think you do."

With one quick pull on my hip, he rolled me onto my stomach. His hand came down on my butt with a loud crack.

"You trapped me, Blue."

Smack.

Ow! These weren't playful swats, and it stung.

I tried to wriggle away, but he only spanked me again.

"Ford!"

"Not with a baby. We'll make a baby. Someday. When you're ready. But you trapped me with that sass. Those blue eyes. With everything about you. Consider me good and taken."

He spanked me again.

As quick as he began, it was over, and he turned me right back over. He brushed my hair out of my face.

"Taken by you. Got me, Indigo Buchanan? I *want* to be trapped."

God, this man. He wanted me. *Me!*

He was a SEAL. Fought in a war. Talented. Skilled. Gorgeous. He could have any woman in the world. Maybe he'd had a few of them, but somehow, he'd come back to our tiny Montana town to settle and wanted me.

My eyes filled with tears, and I nodded.

He studied me then nodded too. Moving off of me, he stood again and shucked his clothes.

"Be a good girl, Blue, and get rid of that top, then tell me what you want."

"You," I whispered, wiping my eye with my thumb. I wasn't going to cry. Not when the most perfect male specimen was getting naked before me as I pulled the tank top over my head.

He shook his head, and I noticed his hair was a little longer. His beard needed a trim. "Not good enough. You've got me." He gripped the base of his cock and began to stroke it. Completely uninhibited and with zero modesty. Although someone who looked like him should be proud of himself. "I don't want to think."

His hand stilled. "If you're thinking while we're fucking, we're not doing it right. Here's how this is going to go, so you know upfront. So you can stop thinking."

I licked my lips in anticipation.

"I've gotten my cum down that throat and marked that pussy. I'm going to take your ass tonight."

That was not what I'd expected him to say. I clenched involuntarily at what he planned. "Um..."

"You soak my dick when I play with that virgin hole. You clench and milk my dick. Don't deny you like me touching you there." He leaned down, wrapped an arm behind my back and hoisted me up the bed then settled himself over me.

His skin was so hot, the muscles so hard. So was his dick, and it had only been a few minutes since he'd come. He kissed me, slow and savoring. The feel of his beard against my face was soft. When his lips traced the line of my jaw, I angled my head. He murmured in my ear. "The other day, when you rolled onto your stomach to show me what you wanted, you wanted more than just a pussy fuck, didn't you?"

I blinked up at my ceiling, then moaned when his head drifted lower, so he could latch onto my nipple. His nose nudged my necklace. My fingers tangled in his hair. "Ford," I breathed.

"Didn't you?" he repeated. "Whatever you need, Blue."

Did I want that? Something so dark and intimate, something so... carnal? That first time, when I'd done as he'd said, he'd told me he'd get a finger in my ass first, then his dick. He'd done exactly what he'd said, and I'd loved it. Pressed up against the door just a few minutes ago, I'd come so hard because he'd breached me there.

I did like it, and I could feel the nerve endings still firing. I had no idea it would feel so good. It had been a fantasy, a naughty longing, but I never expected to find a man who'd fulfill it without me feeling like a... oh my God. A slut.

But Ford was right there with me. Giving it to me

because it was something he'd known I'd like. He'd tested me to see, somehow knowing how far to push me. To give me what I wanted. No, needed. He wasn't making me out to be a slut for wanting him to fuck my ass. He was going to share this desire with me because he wanted it too.

"I... yes."

His teeth raked over my nipple, then he lifted his head. Gave me a smile, something he rarely shared with anyone. "Good girl. Gotta do this right. Got any lube?"

"No. I have coconut oil in the bathroom."

He arched a brow in response.

"I use it instead of lotion on my face. I put it in my hair sometimes to condition it. It's all natural." I had no idea why I was rambling and selling the stuff to Ford.

He shifted to his side to allow me up. "Go and spoon some into a little bowl and bring it here."

I shivered as I raced to the kitchen then the bathroom following his orders. God, were we doing this? His cum slipped from my pussy and slid down my thigh. Yeah, we were doing this.

"I can see you thinking too hard from here," he said.

I set the bowl on the bedside table before

crawling onto the bed. He flopped onto his back with his lower legs off the bed, knees bent and feet on the floor.

"Sit on my face, Blue."

I took in his rock-hard body. His dick curved upward to his belly, but at those words, my gaze flew up to his.

He crooked a finger.

"But, I... you, I'm dripping," I admitted.

That smile appeared again. "Just the way I like you."

"With your cum, Ford," I countered.

He sighed, reached out and lifted me. Yes, lifted me. I straddled his upper torso.

"Higher," he growled.

He wasn't squishy or grossed out that his cum was dripping from me. I didn't move, slightly embarrassed, but the smack on my right butt cheek had me gasping and crawling up, so I hovered over his face.

"Fuck, you smell good. I love knowing I've been inside you, that I've marked you."

He didn't say anything else, just used his big mountain man hands to pull me down onto his mouth. I set my hands on the bed in front of me as he—

"Oh my God," I shouted.

He was licking up everything that slipped from me, then he found my clit with his wicked tongue. I felt fingers slipping through the wetness, then a finger... no, a thumb, curve and press into my ass.

I clenched and came. It hadn't even been a minute, but I hadn't been thinking, just feeling.

I hadn't been thinking.

My skin was sweaty, my breathing ragged. I was wilted, and my clit tingled and pulsed. My head hung down, and I felt so, so good.

"Ford," I whispered, my voice hoarse.

I kept my eyes closed but felt him move, sliding down the bed and out from beneath me. I flopped down onto the bed, my knees bent underneath me.

"Stay just like that," he said.

"Mmm," I muttered into the blanket.

A big hand stroked down my back as I felt fingers cupping my pussy, gently sliding over the tender flesh.

I gasped and startled, my body so sensitive.

"Shh, lots of oil."

The bed pressed down by my knees, letting me know—besides his fingers on me—where he was.

His fingers were so slick, and the tropical scent of the coconut oil mixed with the musky tang of sex.

After he worked me back up, his fingers moved to my ass and circled, then pressed.

I felt a hand press into the bed by my head, the heated contact of his chest against my back as he murmured in my ear. "You took my finger so well. I'm going to take my time now, get you good and ready. Lots of the oil. Soon you'll be begging."

I wasn't sure about that, but Ford wasn't touching me in any way I didn't like. His fingers caressed me and stroked my body possessively. Reverently. Yet it was naughty. Filthy, the way he was circling, then pressing a finger in, working it shallow at first, then deeper. When I felt the stretch was too much, he receded completely, collecting more coconut oil for another slide into me. First it was one finger, then two.

I rolled my hips, pushed my hips back as he kept at it. I didn't know how much time had passed or what was going on outside this room, outside the two of us. Of his fingers in me. Playing. Taunting.

"Ford," I moaned, then came up onto my elbows.

I heard his chuckle.

"See? Begging." He kissed down the line of my spine. "Tell me what you want, Blue."

I pressed my face into the mattress and shook my head. "You know what I want!"

"Need you to say it, baby. Tell me you want me to fuck your virgin ass."

Oh God. It was one thing for me to present my butt to him, to even bring him the coconut oil as an offering for him to work me open. All of that was telling him exactly what I wanted. Now he wanted more.

"I want everything, Indigo Buchanan. Give me all of you, and I'll give you my dick. It's so fucking hard for you. You're so sweet. So dirty like this I'm not going to last. I'll give you my cum. I'll mark your ass as mine."

"Fuck me, Ford. Fuck my ass," I whispered.

"Such a good, naughty girl," he replied, and his fingers slipped from me, and I heard some rustling, then the press of his dick against my back entrance.

I was so slick, but I knew he'd coated himself with even more oil, protecting me from it being too rough. He pressed against me, then back, then again.

"Deep breath. Good girl. Let it out."

With that instruction, I relaxed, and the flared head of his dick breached me, my body giving up the fight.

I winced at the twinge of pain, but it was a full-ness that had me gasping.

"You good, baby?"

I nodded then swallowed hard. "Yes."

He pressed forward only a fraction, then back, doing that again and again as his hand slid up and down my back until the last pass when his hand cupped the back of my neck and tangled in my hair.

He held me down. Not that I was going to go anywhere, but the feel of him holding me in place so he could fuck my ass was so hot.

"Ford," I moaned as he fucked me slowly and carefully. He felt even bigger back there, that he was going impossibly deeper until his hips bumped my bottom.

"Look at you," he murmured. "Taking all of my dick. Your ass is perfect stretched around me."

A finger circled around my taut flesh, and I cried out. Arched my back. Him being inside me was one thing, but the nerve endings were on the outside.

"Ford!" I cried, then pushed back.

"Like that?" He bent all the way over me and fucked me harder. "Taking my dick like a good girl. So deep. Not a virgin any longer, Blue. This ass is mine. Fuck, clench like that again, and I'm going to fill you right up. You'll have two holes dripping my cum for—"

I did just that. Clenched down on him, and he groaned.

One of his hands came between me and the bed and found my clit.

"Naughty girl," he growled. "Time for you to come all filled with dick."

With those filthy words, he pinched my clit. Pinched the hell out of it, and I came.

I screamed, tried to writhe, but he held me down too well.

He fucked me harder. Deeper. Once, twice, then I felt him swell and then pulse in me.

Ford's groan was dark and feral, and I knew he'd lost himself in me.

I wasn't the only one who forgot to think. To be lost to everything but us.

"Ford," I breathed, then I let go. Completely.

CHAPTER
FOURTEEN

FORD

THE NEXT MORNING, after spending a solid hour working Indi's body over a few times until she was hoarse from screaming and drunk on orgasms, we walked into town to grab coffee at the Seed n' Feed.

Ass fucking was probably every guy's fantasy, but it hadn't been like that. Her consent meant she trusted me enough to allow me to do it. That she was right there with me, that she came so hard that she practically strangled my dick? Fuck, it had been the most amazing connection.

I was lost in her. Obsessed. I'd tucked her into

the shower when we were done to clean up then I found her a bag of frozen peas. Yeah, a fucking bag of peas because my dick was big, and that ass had been tight... and virgin. I'd fallen asleep holding her, knowing that she trusted me so implicitly, yet I was still holding back...

Fuck. So what that I'd given her so much pleasure and satisfaction this morning. I knew I was holding back information she'd want to know. Holding back anything felt like a betrayal after all she'd given me. All she let me in.

The farm supply store and now coffee shop was in the center of town—an old red brick building from the turn of the century, like the rest of the town center. Sparks was small, but what it lacked in size, it made up for in quaint beauty. A large roundabout with a park and fountain in the middle allowed for cruising Main Street on weekends, and there was no place you could stand and not see the spectacular mountain views.

Hanging flower baskets dangled from the vintage street lights. It was picture perfect, and it made no sense why all I'd wanted to do was leave this place.

Maybe a few tours in a war zone made me realize exactly what I'd had all along. Same went for the woman beside me.

"Well, hello, you two," Holly said brightly when we walked in. Gram had told me she was the one who came up with the idea to convert part of the building into a little coffee shop. Pure genius. Her gaze traveled between Indi and I with curiosity.

We placed our order for one coffee and one mocha. When Holly returned with them, she shamelessly asked, "So, are you two a thing now?"

That was a small town for you. Everybody's business was everybody's business. Which was one of the reasons I had kept to myself up on the family property by the mountain since I returned. I hadn't wanted to talk about why I'd left the military, and I especially didn't want to talk about Buck.

But I had no problem setting the record straight on this issue. I slid my arm around the front of Indi and pulled her ass back against my front. "Yep. We are definitely a thing." In Indi's ear, I murmured, "You're *my* thing."

"Wow." Holly chuckled in surprise. "That's a fun development. You know, Buck would be happy, I'm sure."

I almost managed not to wince. Buck was still a sore topic and not just for me. I tightened my hold on Indi in case she felt the same elevator drop every time she heard his name.

"I'll bet your parents are thrilled," Holly said, looking to Indi.

"Ah, they don't know yet," Indi said, twisting to look over her shoulder at me. "But I'm sure they will soon."

Unease churned in my belly. Would Buck's and Indi's parents be thrilled? They sure as hell hadn't wanted to see me after the memorial service. Of course, I hadn't wanted to see myself either, so we were in agreement on that. It had been a dark time.

I dropped two fives on the counter and picked up my coffee. "Keep the change."

"Thanks," Holly offered with a megawatt smile. "Have a great day."

As we walked out, Indi darted another glance my way. "We're going to be the talk of the town in about an hour."

"That long?" We fell into step with each other on the sidewalk. It had rained sometime during the night, and the concrete was drying in places. The air had a hint of dampness, as if everything was washed clean. "If the town's going to be gabbing about me, I love it with your name attached," I declared. "But your parents?"

"Yes?"

"Will they—are they—" I cleared my throat. "Have they forgiven me?"

Indi stopped and faced me. Her hair was back in a ponytail, and she wore no makeup and was hands down the prettiest thing I'd ever seen in my life. She put her hands on her hips. "Ford, what are you talking about?"

I worked to swallow. Sweat broke out on my upper lip, and I wanted to run and not stop.

"For Buck's death?" she asked.

I managed to nod.

"What is there to forgive?" She studied my face closely. A little too closely. "Were you part of it? Whatever got him killed?"

"No." Thank God I didn't have to lie about that. I hadn't been a part of that. No fucking way. But I had been there. I felt responsible. "Your mom told me it was too painful to see me after his death. That's why I haven't been around. But it's... eaten at me, you know?" I scrubbed a hand across my beard. "It feels wrong, and I don't know how to make it right. The only way to do that is if Buck would come back. But he won't."

"Come on." Indi tugged my arm. "Let's go see them now. It's time to get past that."

Relief that Indi believed we could move on had

me following at her side. We cut through an alleyway to head toward the south part of town where Buchanan Lumber and Hardware store stood.

Just the sight of it made my chest hurt. I had so damn many memories tied up with the place. The sound of the bell on the door when it opened. The smell of fresh sawdust and popcorn from the machine that stood in the corner, always full with fresh, buttered kernels for the patrons.

Buck and I used to stop in on the way home from school to fill our bellies with popcorn. Indi would often be there, too, perched behind the counter to do her homework.

The familiar bell jangled as we entered.

Sam Buchanan looked over from the counter where he was ringing up an old timer, and he did a double-take when he saw my hand on Indi's lower back. After saying goodbye to his customer, he cocked his head as the two of us approached.

"Morning, Mr. Buchanan." Fuck, if I didn't feel like an errant seventeen-year-old. One who was about to knock on the Buchanan's door to take their daughter out on a first date.

Only we'd already had a first date, second and third date. Sam Buchanan might as well grab his shotgun because I'd fully sullied his—

No, no. She was an adult. We were both adults now. And we weren't living in the 1950s when fathers chased boys with shotguns.

"Morning Ford. Hi, Indi."

Seemed like he said it extra loud, so his wife, Page, would hear. Sure enough, she poked her head out of the office. Everything was so familiar, so like the old times, that it hurt.

"Ford. Hello. Hi, sweetheart." There was a question in her voice. Something like, *what the hell are you doing with our daughter?*

"Everything all right? Your place didn't get broken into again, did it?" Sam asked, his gaze shifting from me to focus on Indi.

"Roger Mellman's getting the help he needs, and everything's back to normal," she said.

"No, no," I added, shaking my head. "We have that place tighter than a drum now. No one will bother Indi over there."

Indi nestled herself up against my side and put a claiming hand on my chest. "Ford is taking good care of me."

"Oh." Page sounded startled. Her hair was fair like Indi's but cut short. She had on jeans and a pale blue shirt, with the hardware store's green apron over top.

"That right?" Sam asked. His hair had turned grayer since I'd seen him at the memorial service. "I didn't even know you two were...*reacquainted* since Ford's been back."

"Well, I got caught in a storm hiking and had to take refuge at his place, and well... yeah. We're more than reacquainted now." She glanced up at me, a smile pulling at her lips.

I loved the look she gave me, but it wasn't reassuring. Why was this so fucking awkward?

It was like all my shame and guilt over Buck's death rendered me stupid. I could face down the enemy without even blinking. I'd been trained and trained on handling any kind of stressful situation. To think on the fly. To respond.

Except in this. Not one fucking second of my time with the SEALs had given me the skills to handle the grieving parents of my best friend.

"I'm sorry I haven't been by more," I burst out, determined to address the issue. "I should've been, you know? I just...wasn't sure how welcome I was."

"Oh Ford!" Page came out of the office, circling the counter to come and throw her arms around me. She was small like Indi, and her head pressed into my chest. "That was my fault. I shouldn't have said what I did. I was wrong. It wasn't painful to see you.

Everything was painful. I've hated that it kept you away." Tears clogged her voice, while she patted my back like we were still family.

I banded my arms around her back and held her as I glanced at Indi—who'd stepped back—and Sam. "No, I get it. It's been hell for all of us. Not a day goes by where something doesn't make me think of Buck and I don't still feel the ache of losing him."

Sam cleared his throat. He'd come out from behind the counter, too, and had given Indi a kiss on the cheek. "We don't want you to feel unwelcome, Ford." He offered his hand for me to shake. "You're as much a son to us as Buck was." He choked up, too.

I clasped his hand in mine, my eyes smarting. I cleared the rust from my throat. "Thank you. I, uh, I have some extra wood split for winter, and I'd like to bring it by."

Sam's face split into a grin. "We'd appreciate that, Ford."

"And we'd like to have you two over for dinner soon," Page said. "We'll text Indi with a date. How does that sound?"

"Sounds great," I said, feeling like an eighty pound pack had been lifted from my shoulders.

"Yes, that would be nice," Indi agreed. "I have a

guide trip this week, but maybe we could do it when I get home."

"Sounds like a plan," Page said, giving me another hug.

Sam shook my hand again, and Indi kissed both her parents.

When I escorted her out of the hardware store, she tipped her face up to me with a soft smile. "See? No one blames you for what happened. We love you, Ford. All of us."

I caught Indi around the waist and pulled her against me. A woman with a dog on a leash passed us, but she could have had two heads for how much attention I was giving her. It was horrible SEAL behavior, not constantly aware of one's surroundings, but Indi had said the words.

The words.

"Did you just say you love me?"

She gave a nervous laugh then glanced away. "Maybe."

I kissed her nose and turned her face back to mine. "Go on, say it for real. You love me. Say it."

She blinked up at me. "I love you," she murmured.

My heart shot to the sky like a rocket then parachuted down, twirling and dancing in the breeze. I never imagined in a million years that I'd hear those words from this woman. That my life would do a complete one-fucking-eighty in the span of a few weeks.

There was only one thing I could do—since fucking her six ways to Sunday wasn't happening on the sidewalk—was to say it right back.

"I love you, Indigo Buchanan."

CHAPTER
FIFTEEN

INDI

AFTER WORKING in the SOA office the next day, I headed out of town to Ford's place. In the course of just a few weeks, he'd become my new habit. My joy. My everything.

I was leaving tomorrow for the guide trip, and I wanted to soak up every last minute with him before I went.

I parked on the gravel drive in front of the main house. Roscoe barked from somewhere else on the property as I headed up the steps to knock on the door. It was the first time I'd been over here since the storm, and now I noticed what good repair everything was in. There was a new roof on the main house and fresh paint. The wooden porch looked freshly stained and sealed. There was drip irrigation installed all along Mrs. L's flowerbeds, and the five giant pine trees that stood in front of the house had some lower branches trimmed and their cuts sealed.

The guys were obviously taking good care of Ford's grandma.

Mrs. L answered the door at the same time Roscoe ran up behind me, wagging and licking my hand when I greeted him by name.

"Hi, Indi. How are you doing, honey?" She gave me her usual smile as she wiped her hand on a dish-towel. The scent of brownies hit me and made my mouth water.

I leaned in to give the spry old woman a hug. "Great. Is Ford around?" I glanced in the direction Roscoe had come from, guessing that's where I'd find him.

"The guys are up in the greenhouse. It's their training room now, you know."

"Ah yes, the training room." I wouldn't mind watching a little of that training. Especially if it involved Ford taking off his shirt and flexing all those powerful muscles. "I'll just head over there, then. Thanks."

Roscoe and I walked to the greenhouse, and I pushed the door open. This time it wasn't locked, and I saw the window I'd broken to get in had been replaced. I wasn't disappointed by what I found. Four very hot Navy SEALs working out. Of course, my gaze was immediately drawn to my mountain man. Ford was doing chin-ups on a bar attached to the back wall, the muscles of his arms and back flexing in perfect coordinated rhythm with each surge upward.

Taft was on his back on a bench in the center of the room pressing iron. Hayes was doing pushups on an incline, and Kennedy had on sparring gloves and was working over the punching bag.

Ford looked over his shoulder without pausing in his routine. "Hey, Blue." His eyes crinkled with more warmth than I ever imagined I'd see in the guy.

I tried not to swoon. Or jump him.

"Hey, Indi!" Hayes panted. Kennedy waved. Taft set the weights down on the rack and sat up.

"Don't stop on my account," I said. "I don't mind the show."

"Hey. Eyes over here," Ford demanded, and I chuckled. "I'm almost finished," he added.

"Don't rush," I said, trying not to drool. "Seriously, take all the time you need. I'll join you guys."

Carrying heavy packs and paddling rafts down the river kept me in excellent shape, but I enjoyed working out in a gym now and again.

I walked over to where Taft sat and picked a kettlebell from the shelf. I held it in both hands between my legs to do my squats. He was in shorts, and I could see the angry scar that ran from the outside of his calf past his left knee and part way up his thigh.

"Gunshot wound," he said, answering my unasked question. "Put me out of the SEALs with a medical discharge." He flashed a rueful smile, but I knew he had to be faking it. I pegged him a few years younger than me, so he'd barely been in the service before he'd been forced out.

My heart ached for him, and I pushed away the thoughts of what he'd been up to—and had to endure—to be shot. I had to believe he'd been as dedicated and gung-ho about his military career as Buck and Ford had been. "Getting sidelined has to suck," I commiserated.

He smirked and grabbed his water bottle off the floor by his feet. "Yeah. Getting the call from Ford to come join his security company pretty much made my year."

"I'll bet." I set the kettlebell down to rest for a moment.

He squeezed the plastic bottle and water shot into his mouth like a fountain. "But being on the team without Ford sucked, too," he said after he swallowed. "When he was dishonorably discharged over Buck, we all wanted to quit on the spot."

Ice cold washed over me, and I was glad I wasn't holding the weight or I'd have dropped it on my foot. "Dishonorably discharged?" My stomach seized up in a tight knot. Why hadn't I heard anything about this? What the hell? I flicked my gaze at Ford. "Over Buck?"

Taft's eyes flew wide, and he had a panicked look. One that hadn't appeared when he'd told me about being shot, but when he'd obviously stuck his booted foot in his mouth. "Oh shit...I mean...uh... you didn't know that part?"

My body started shaking like a leaf. "What part? What happened? Tell me now."

From the corner of my eye, I saw Ford take note of my tone and drop. He prowled my way.

"No, no. It's not what you think," Taft backpedaled. All the guys stopped what they were doing. The tension in the room ratcheted up. "I mean, I don't know what you think, but he wasn't involved. Ford didn't cause Buck's death. He was looking into it. Because we all know what they said he did was bogus, right?"

Taft looked around for help from his teammates.

I caught Kennedy making the throat cut gesture to shut him up.

What the *actual* fuck?

I whirled to face Ford. "You were dishonorably discharged." I was reeling. He'd been keeping things from me. Things that pertained to him. To Buck's death.

He held his hands out. "Hang on, Blue. Why are you upset?"

"I'm upset because you've been keeping this from me." I threw my arms wide. "All of this." I paced away to get my temper under control and saw Kennedy tipping his head at the other two, and they bolted for the door.

I waited until the three left the greenhouse— Kennedy whispering a *Nice job, dumbass* to Taft on the way out—before I lit into Ford again.

"Why were you dishonorably discharged?" I crossed my arms over my chest.

Ford's jaw clenched. "Officially? Failing a urine test. Which was bullshit. But I believe it's because I wouldn't stop asking questions about Buck's death. We're going to figure it out, Indi. The team is on it."

I blinked and tried to figure out who this man was. If he was the same one who'd been with me the night before. Said he loved me. But this? This wasn't love.

"You're... looking into Buck's death? What happened to *Buck's gone. Nothing we do will bring him back?*"

Ford opened his mouth then shut it again. Yeah, he couldn't answer that. "Okay." He cocked his head to the side and spread his hands in placation. "Listen. I didn't want you poking into it, Blue. It could be dangerous. Buck would kill me if I put you into danger."

I dropped my head back with frustration and stared up at the glass ceiling. We were full circle. Meeting in the greenhouse after all these years, arguing. Starting things up.

It seemed we'd be arguing and ending it all right here too.

"Oh, great. Here's Buck in the middle of our relationship again. And I'm just the kid sister who needs protection. Thanks a whole fucking lot, Ford!"

I wasn't usually into drama, but I needed time to

cool off and think about this, so I whirled on my heel to march out.

"Hang on." Ford caught my elbow and tugged me back, which only further angered me.

"Let go!" I snapped, and his hand instantly sprang free.

"Whoa." He held his palms up once more. "Sorry. Fuck, please don't go. Let's talk this out."

"Talk this out? *Talk this out?* No, Ford. You had your chance for talking when you saw my bulletin board. You chose to keep me out of it when you knew how much it meant to me. You could've told me the truth, to give me hope that Buck wasn't—" I couldn't finish that sentence. I took a deep breath. "So no, we're not going to talk this out right now. I'm leaving. I'm not sure when or if I'll get over this."

"Indi!" Ford called to my retreating back.

Roscoe whined.

I flipped him the bird as I made my way to the open door.

Damn him.

Damn Ford and his high-handed, big brotherly bullshit.

I stopped to turn just outside. "I'm leaving for my guide trip. While I'm away, you need to choose—are you my man or are you my big brother? Because you sure as hell can't be both." With that, I marched out, my fingers balled into fists.

"Indi!" Ford shouted again, but I ignored him, beelining it for my 4Runner.

I got behind the wheel and drove off with Roscoe chasing me, barking as if he knew his master didn't want me to go.

———

FORD

DAMMIT.

Things were too new with Indi for me to know whether or not I just completely lost her or could fight my way back from this.

No, fuck that. I wouldn't lose her. I would definitely fight for her. For us. I'd fight until she believed in me.

She'd given me an ultimatum. She didn't say she was done completely. That part gave me a sliver of hope.

Still, the pain that lanced through my chest was almost as sharp as the pain of losing Buck. To think that yesterday I thought maybe I could have it all, and today, everything crashed and burned so catastrophically.

It had been wrong to keep all this from her. Indi was right—she deserved better. She must feel patronized and underestimated right now.

Fuck—maybe she felt that same rejection I'd served her with when she'd shown up in my bedroom years ago. Because I'd pretty much rejected her for my friendship with Buck. I could have had Indi that night, had the most incredible time with her, but Buck would have hated my fucking guts.

Looking back, we hadn't been ready then. It would have been one time and nothing more because I couldn't have stayed. The US government had been my employer. I couldn't disobey orders and just quit. AWOL wasn't an option. Deep down, I'd done the right thing.

But the price of that rejection had been solely Indi's. She'd seen it as that. Being turned down because she wasn't enough. I'd had to choose between her and the military with her brother.

I'd chosen the military.

Now? Now... I chose her and solely because the military had kicked me out. She was the only good thing that had come from the fucking double-cross. No. Not the only thing. I'd thought returning to

Sparks was like being exiled. But it was a new life. A *better* life. With Indi.

So yeah, I chose her. Even if my name was cleared and I was invited back, this time, I wouldn't go. I wouldn't leave her again.

But I had. Because I technically hadn't left. My head was still caught up on the fuck-all of Buck's death. Of my discharge. And I wouldn't be free to belong to Indi outright, to give her everything that I was until I was cleared.

I ran a hand over the back of my neck, tugged on my hair that was getting too fucking long.

No. That wasn't true. All I had to do was tell her what we were up to. Why the guys were here working for me and my security business not only for a post-military life—because we all wanted justice for Buck. She'd have let us do our SEAL, mountain man shit.

I should've given her everything.

While she'd literally gotten on her hands and knees for me, submitting in the most intimate of ways, I'd still held back.

I was a fucking asshole.

I pulled out my phone to text her. *I'm your man. No more big-brothering. I'm sorry, Blue. Can we talk?*

I stood there like a dumbass watching my phone and waiting for her to reply, but she didn't.

Blowing out my breath, I trudged back to the greenhouse. I would need at least three more hours of chin-ups to keep me from running after her, busting down her door and pinning her to a wall until I figured out the right thing to say to make her forgive me.

But I knew that wasn't what she needed at the moment. I had to give her space and time to cool off. I'd texted, and she hadn't responded. I would try again in a few hours.

Fuck.

If she went into the wilderness without us getting this resolved, I was going to go apeshit.

Oh, the irony was so fucking sweet because this was exactly what I'd done to her. We argued and left her to go off to war nine years ago.

Payback was a fucking bitch.

With a curse, I jumped for the chin up bar and heaved my bodyweight up to get my head over it. One...two...three...

Fuck.

CHAPTER
SIXTEEN

INDI

I WAS LESS fuming and more hurt by the time I got home. I wasn't sure if this was an all-out breakup moment for me and Ford, but it certainly seemed like a huge red flag.

I wasn't going to date a guy who still treated me like a kid sister. I just wasn't.

That one night all those years ago had destroyed us in so many ways. I'd been in love with Ford back then. I might have been bold enough to climb naked into his bed, but I wouldn't have done that for any guy. His rejection had stung. No, it had destroyed me.

Except I hadn't known what hurt was really like until Buck died. And now, when I thought being with Ford was healing both wounds, I'd been completely wrong. He didn't trust me with the truth. Didn't think I was an equal. That I was the woman for him because he expected me to stand behind him instead of by his side.

I ignored the texts Ford sent and focused on getting ready for my trip. I watered my houseplants, packed my bags and took a long, hot bath.

I climbed out of the tub and dried off. I must've been too rough with the towel because I somehow tugged on the necklace Buck gave me. It broke and clattered on the tile floor.

"Fuck," I muttered, staring down at it. Well, that was adding insult to injury. Like I needed any more painful reminders of Buck's death today.

I bent down and picked up the pendant, which now had a loose centerpiece. I tried to reset the blue stone, but it wouldn't lie flat. It was broken.

Dammit.

Grief welled as I studied it. This had been the last thing I'd received from Buck. The last gift that he'd taken the time to pick out for me. It was a weird gift choice since I didn't really wear jewelry, but the stone color wasn't lost on me. If he hadn't died just a few weeks later, I probably would've set it on my dresser and saved it to wear only when he came home.

But he *had* died, and it felt like I still had this little piece of him. Like he'd sent it ahead of time to comfort me through the shock and grief of his death. I'd put it on the day we were told and hadn't taken it off since.

I brought the pendant closer to inspect the loose stone. I used my fingernail to pry it up, and the damn thing sprang up, dropping onto the bathroom floor.

"Buck," I croaked because at this point it felt like he was trying to tell me something. Maybe that I was a fucking mess or that things with Ford were going to fall apart, too?

I knelt on the bathmat to collect the stone, but there was something else that had fallen. I picked up what looked like an SD card. A small memory card that stored pictures and files that were kept on a phone. I drew in a shocked breath.

"Buck!"

My hands shook as I held it in front of my eyes to inspect. Oh my God! Buck hadn't sent me a necklace to wear! He'd sent some kind of information. To me. *Me!*

But what?

I threw on a sleep shirt and panties and dashed to my laptop to put the chip into the reader.

I was half-terrified of what I would find. *Please tell me Buck wasn't a spy.*

Or a drug dealer.

Or a murderer.

Please let this be something—anything—that explained his death.

I waited as the computer pulled up the card's window. There was only one file in it. I double-clicked, and it opened a low-resolution video. The footage was shaky, and the room was dim, so it took me a moment to realize what I was watching. Until I heard Buck's deep voice speaking Farsi, at least I thought it was Farsi. And then I realized the footage was filmed from his point of view—like a bodycam or some such device. From the angle, it must've been attached to Buck's torso. Added somewhere on his gear.

An Afghan man in a uniform was tied to a chair. A US soldier stood in front of him with a gun pointed in the center of the guy's head.

I felt sick, and my heart was frantic. This was real. Not a TV or movie. This had actually happened. Buck was questioning the prisoner, and the man was responding in pleading, urgent tones. He tried to look around the soldier with the gun to Buck. His face was bloodied and swollen, and he appeared afraid, like they'd been torturing him.

I drew back, shocked and disgusted. Was this what our government had done over there?

And then I screamed.

Because the soldier shot the prisoner right through the head. CGI or special effects were very realistic because I... oh my God.

"What the fuck?" Buck barked in English.

"Make it look like an accident," a commanding voice said from off-screen.

"This isn't right," Buck replied. I could hear the shock in his voice. "What the fuck? This was to get intel not *kill* the guy. What the hell are we doing here? We can't—"

"You listen to me." The camera was suddenly obscured by camouflage material, like the speaker was so close to Buck the mystery man had his hands on him.

I heard the scrape of Buck's breath and muffled sounds like the mic was being knocked around.

"This is US government business here. It's not for you to question what's right and what's not.

You're here to do a fucking job, do you understand me?"

Buck's breath continued to heave, and he didn't answer for a moment. "You can't fucking do this. The drug investigation you had me ask him about—"

"What in the fuck did I just tell you?" The guy snarled. "It's none of your goddamn business. Are you going to keep your mouth shut, or are we digging two graves today? Trust me, sailor, I have no problem leaving you here. It would make it easy to hang that man's death on you, so your family doesn't get a penny of your death benefits. Is that what you want?"

After a long pause, Buck dragged in a breath and said, "No, sir."

"Then shut up and help Tully get rid of the body."

"Yes, sir."

The video showed dizzying movement accompanied by Buck's still frenzied breath as he moved toward the body, and then it cut out.

Oh my God. Was that the murder that had been pinned on him? It had to have been if he'd been worried about it enough to send me the memory card of it before he died.

The threat had been plain. Whoever had been

speaking could have simply carried out his threat a few weeks later.

Did that mean they'd killed more than one local? Why? It had something to do with drugs.

I sat back in my chair and closed my eyes, willing the nausea the video had ignited to calm down.

I had the report of the man's death on my bulletin board. Knew his name and now knew exactly how he'd died.

"Buck," I moaned aloud. God, my poor brother. Trapped into something terrible that went against his moral code, and he'd tried to do the right thing. Clearly, he'd taken the video in secret. The guy in charge, the one who'd hassled him, hadn't known it was recorded. Then Buck had sent me the evidence for safekeeping. Because it had been important enough to sneak out in a gift for me.

I gasped, slapping my hand over my mouth. That was why Buck's last words to Ford were about protecting me! He wasn't just playing big brother! He was trying to tell Ford I had the evidence!

Ford recognized the necklace. He'd said they'd been together when Buck had bought it at a local bazaar. Ford hadn't mentioned anything about hiding something inside. He hadn't known. Sure, he'd been lying to me, but he'd have snagged it off my neck first thing if he'd been aware. Buck had kept Ford in the dark too.

Goosebumps raced along my arms, and I got up to pace.

There were at least three members of the US military in the video. Buck, some commanding officer whose face I never saw, and the guy, Tully.

Were they part of the Army Ranger team Buck had been pulled onto before he died? The guy called Tully had a slightly different uniform than the ones I'd seen Buck wearing in pictures he'd emailed. Was that important? I had no idea.

I sped back to my desk chair when an idea occurred to me. Pulling up Facebook, I searched for Army Ranger Tully.

My heart leaped to my throat when it produced a few results... but one had a face I recognized from the dim video.

That man, Cameron Tully from Russell Shoals, Texas, was the real killer—not Buck. Maybe he'd set the bomb in Buck's Jeep, not the enemy.

So what had Buck been doing the day he got killed? Had he been lured to his death by someone on that team? Because I sure as hell knew he wasn't buying drugs.

Tears stung my eyes thinking how Buck must've

suffered emotionally leading up to his death. That murder would've weighed on his conscience. I'm guessing he'd known something was off from the beginning of that recorded interview, or he wouldn't have activated his camera.

Or maybe they always had them on, what did I know?

Ford might have answers about that. Except he didn't because he didn't know. He'd said the guys were looking into it, into clearing Buck's record and even his own. They'd have done it by now if successful.

My irritation with Ford was still fresh, but he needed this video. He'd know what to do with it. This wasn't something I could figure out on my own. This wasn't searching online and writing to people in the military about my dead brother.

God, that video was... evil.

I took the tiny memory card out of my computer and dropped it in an envelope, along with the pieces of the necklace, in case they were relevant. I sealed it and wrote Ford's name on the front.

I couldn't handle talking to him tonight— between our fight and this sickening revelation, I didn't have anything left in me. I'd go to bed and drop the envelope by Ford's place in the morning before I went out on the trip.

Whether he and I worked out our differences, Ford needed to see the truth. I owed Buck that much.

CHAPTER
SEVENTEEN

FORD

I HADN'T HEARD from Indi. It'd almost been two days. Two days of radio silence. Of life like before she'd busted into the greenhouse. I'd spent years without her, and then with one pinging sensor on the security system, she'd re-entered my life.

It'd taken me two weeks or so to fuck it up this time.

I'd excluded her when I'd known I shouldn't. I'd done it to protect her, but how safe was she when she wasn't in my arms at night?

After another sleepless night, I climbed from the bed as the sky turned a hint of pink. I threw on my running shoes and headed for the hills, pounding out my frustration and anger over miles of wilderness. I stuck to the edge of Ledger land and the dirt roads around it. I clocked maybe ten miles before turning up the drive, walking the familiar dirt lane, and taking in the place.

This had been the only home I'd really known, even moving here at twelve. It was where I'd found a place to belong. Boundaries. Unconditional love. Motivation. Now, it was a place to return and put down roots. I'd intended for it to be a way for me to watch over Gram and finally be there for her but also as a base for Alpha Mountain.

Except in the morning light, I saw the place differently now. I wanted to make it more than just a base. Gram's house. I wanted it to be mine. There was no way in fuck I'd be with Indi and sleep down the hall from my grandmother. Not in the bunkhouse either. Her cries of pleasure as I ate her out were for my ears only. I wanted her to be able to walk around in just a t-shirt and sexy little panties without three horny, single SEALs around every corner. My cabin would be finished in the next few months down by the creek. We'd live there. If I could get in front of Indi and explain. Grovel.

After my shower, I came down the back steps to the scent of bacon.

"Morning, dear," Gram said. She had tongs in her hands. The back door was open, and Roscoe was at her feet. He turned to me, then spun back around and plunked down again, eyes on the stove for any chance of getting a meaty treat.

"Morning," I replied.

"I'm surprised Indi's car isn't here," she said, glancing out the window.

I ran a hand over my beard as I opened the fridge and pulled out the milk. I was ready to drink right from the jug, but I received a withering look. Grabbing a glass, I poured it full.

"Indi's off on a guide trip," I commented.

"Good weather," she replied.

I took a few gulps of the cold drink and wiped my mouth and beard with the back of my hand. I hated things in my beard. Except for Indi's scent. Eating her out and having that cream caught...

I cleared my throat and turned back to the fridge to cool down my semi as I put the jug away.

"She's mad at me," I said.

"Oh?"

"I kept something a secret from her. Not sure if she'll be back anytime soon."

She turned off the burner and picked up the bacon to set it on a plate lined with paper towels.

"You're a SEAL, and you're going to give up with one argument?"

"I—"

She gave me another look.

"No, ma'am."

"Unless writing Dear John letters is still a thing, you're not on her shit list."

My mouth opened, and she laughed.

"You think I don't know how to swear? I'm surrounded by Navy men after all. Married to one for forty-two years as well."

I scratched the back of my neck. She had a point. More than one. "What do you mean a Dear John letter?"

"I mean that envelope she left for you yesterday."

I perked up at that. My heart skipped a beat, completely unlike every bit of training I had about remaining cool and level-headed.

"Envelope? What is it? When?"

She carried the bacon to the table then turned to the warming drawer and pulled out a bowl of scrambled eggs.

"You didn't see it? There on the counter." She pointed. "Oh, I must've set my grocery sack over it."

I beat her to the cloth bag and handed it to her. Beneath, on the worn laminate, was an envelope with my name on it. I ripped it open and let the contents drop into my hand.

Indi's locket. With the center stone removed. And a... what the fuck?

Gram glanced between me and the contents in my palm with interest.

"Where's Kennedy?" I asked in a low, deadly voice.

She must've recognized the seriousness of my tone because she calmly said, "In the sewing room. I was about to call him for breakfast."

I heard the last of it as I moved, cutting through the lower floor into the temp command center. Kennedy sat in front of his row of monitors, headphones on. He pulled them off when I held my palm up in front of him.

He took the SD card then looked up at me.

"It was in Indi's necklace."

I grabbed a chair and pulled it beside him as he loaded it into a converter port. With a few clicks, a video came up on the screen.

"Holy shit," Kennedy whispered, and I had a really bad fucking feeling about what we were going to see.

"Boys," Gram began, and Kennedy clicked to pause the movie. "The eggs and—"

"I need you to go get Hayes and Taft, Gram. Right now." I didn't look away from the screen.

Thankfully, Gram didn't say a word, and I heard the screen door slam.

Kennedy started the video.

It lasted less than four minutes, but it made everything, *everything,* clear.

"Holy fuck," Kennedy said after it ended.

"Play it again," I said, my blood pumping in my veins. This was how I felt before a mission. Charged, as if I'd been plugged into a light socket.

After we watched it once more, I wasn't sure if I could keep my rage in check.

"This guy... Tully," I breathed. "Get every fucking thing you can on him."

Kennedy nodded, and his fingers flew over the keyboard as the others came in.

Gram must've told them something was up because there was no joking or fooling around. Their expressions were serious. They were ready for whatever we needed.

"I'll let you boys have your space," Gram said. "I'll be at the farmer's market."

When none of us acknowledged her, she slipped

out the back door once more. I was thankful for that woman, and I'd have to make it up to her later, but this was the clue we'd all been waiting for.

"Play it again," I said to Kennedy. He started it up on one of his screens. "That's Buck's camera."

Hayes leaned over Kennedy's shoulder. Taft hovered, his gaze watchful.

"There are two men besides Buck," Taft said. "Tully. The other guy's nameless. And that's Abdul Tareen, the Afghan police officer."

"How do you know for sure?" Hayes asked.

"Rewind," Taft requested. When Kennedy got to the video to a specific spot, he added, "There. There's a scar on his left cheek. Two prongs on the right side where the stitches were."

None of us questioned him. With his photographic memory, if Taft had seen or heard something before, it was fact.

"What about the name Tully?" I asked. "Got anything?"

Taft looked up at the ceiling as if he could find the information there; however, I knew he was searching that encyclopedia of a brain of his. "Cameron Tully, an operative working with Ranger beta team on reconnaissance and security tying to the base infrastructure and alliance with the Afghan people. Assignment ran from June of two years ago until February twenty-seventh of last year. Reassigned to Fort Bragg, North Carolina. Clearance level, confidential."

"What was that data from?" I asked.

Kennedy's fingers were already flying over his keyboard.

"It was in the records you shared with me of all military teams stationed in our quadrant of Afghanistan when we were there. When Buck had died," Taft explained.

That had been a big fucking pile.

"This is him," Kennedy said, enlarging a Department of Defense photo. The video hadn't been the clearest, but this was the guy.

"What about the guy in charge off-camera?" Hayes asked.

"Search any connection between this guy Tully and colleagues within the armed forces. Commanding officers." I looked to Taft. "You and Kennedy work together. Your brain and his machine should give us some results."

"Where'd this come from?" Hayes asked.

"Indi."

Taft and Hayes looked stunned. I grabbed the necklace. "Buck bought this at a bazaar off base with me three weeks before he died. Said the stone color reminded him of Indi. He sent it to her, and it was the last thing she got. She's been wearing it ever since. I guess it broke, and she found the card."

"Holy shit," Hayes said.

"He must've suspected some shady shit to secretly make the recording, but the way he acted in the video, he hadn't expected the guy to be shot. He sent it to his sister for... safe keeping? Or as insurance, if something went wrong," Taft thought out loud.

I nodded. Which it had. "Yet she didn't know she even had it. Didn't even know she carried around something so dangerous about her neck."

"Think she'd have kept it a secret from you? I mean..." Kennedy cut off then scratched his head. Winced.

"Because I didn't share shit with her?" I admitted. "She had that bulletin board. Told me it was nothing but dead ends. No. She must've just broken the necklace recently."

"She hates your guts, man," Hayes added.

I hated the truth, but it was my own fucking fault. I had to own it, at least until I could make it right.

"Yeah, but she loved Buck." I hopped to my feet. "I have to go see her. Now."

"I thought she was on a guide trip," Hayes added.

I nodded, set my hands on my hips. "She is. I'll find out from her boss where she is and head out."

They stared at me wide-eyed.

"What? I'm a fucking SEAL. A hike in the woods is child's play."

Thirty minutes later, I stood across from Brandon, the ex, in the guide office. If I wasn't in such a hurry to get to Indi, to ask her everything she knew about the necklace, and also to apologize, I'd have punched the idiot in the face. This guy was Indi's ex?

"She isn't on the rafting trip," he told me. "I traded her out to take a group up to Glacier Lake."

"Fine, what trail do I take to get there?" I asked.

"I heard you two were together," he countered, crossing his arms. The fucker wasn't answering my damned question. "I don't want your... relationship to mess with the trip."

"Do I look like the kind of man who'd fuck with your business in a way you'd know about?" I countered, my voice low.

He swallowed, then held up his hands. As if they'd protect him.

"Look, man, I told the other guy they're not on a trail."

I stilled. "What other guy?"

"The friend of her brother who insisted he had to see her."

"Friend of Buck?" Every friend of the Buchanan family lived in Sparks.

"How the hell should I know? He was as pushy as you."

I had a bad fucking feeling. My SEAL spidey sense kicked in. I grabbed my cell and called Kennedy. "Text me a pic of the suspect."

I hung up and waited twenty seconds for the image to come through, glaring at Brandon the entire time. I held up the photo of Cameron Tully in front of Brandon's face. "Him? This the family friend?"

Brandon tipped his head back but studied the image. "Yeah man, that's him."

"When did he come by?" I snapped.

"Yesterday afternoon."

Holy fuck. Almost twenty-four hours ago.

"You tell this *friend* where she lived?"

Brandon gave a weak smile. "Well, yeah. He was a friend of Buck's. I thought she'd want to see him."

I was practically seething. If there was a moment

for inner fucking calm, it was right now. I dialed Kennedy again. "He's here and after Indi. I need you three here double time. Bring my gear."

"Hooyah."

I reached across the counter and grabbed the front of Brandon's shirt with my free hand. "Listen to me, you little shit. You gave your employee's home address—your *female* employee—to a total fucking stranger. Then you told him where to find her in the fucking wilderness. You're going to pull out a fucking topo map and show me where they were going."

"Dude, she has GPS. I can pull up her exact location."

With difficulty, I released my hold on him, one tense finger at a time, and he moved quickly to the computer. "There," he said finally, pointing at the screen.

I turned the monitor around, so I could see it. "Print a topo map of this. Where she is, where Glacier Lake is. Then get on the phone and call the sheriff's department and get them mobilized to track down that group. While I'm gone, you're going to shut this fucking business down and move out of Montana, or I swear my SEAL friends and I will kill you as slowly and painfully as we've been trained."

CHAPTER EIGHTEEN

INDI

I NORMALLY LOVED the hike to Glacier Lake. It involved veering off-trail, which meant no other hikers. The entire wilderness to ourselves. Usually my idea of heaven.

This time, though, my mind wouldn't stop looping around Buck and the video. A man's murder. And the way I'd left things with Ford.

In comparison with the bigger picture–the fact that I'd lost my brother because he'd tried to do the right thing in the face of evil–my tiff with Ford now seemed trivial. Like I was a pouting kid.

Did I want to lose him, too? Over me getting my

feathers ruffled for feeling like the left out kid sister again?

No. That was stupid.

Ford may have tried to keep me out of things, but I was in them now. As fully in them as could be. Buck had sent the video to me. He could've handed it to Ford, told him what had been going on, but he hadn't. I'd seen the video, and knowing Ford and his team were on the same side made me feel a whole lot better.

But none of it mattered out here in the back-country. Buck was gone. The video was with Ford. I was five miles from the nearest road. It was only me, nature, and the group I was leading. Turned out, they were amazing. A family of four–a lesbian couple and their two energetic sons, ages eleven and twelve. On trips like this, I packed in the food, so the hikers only had to carry their own personal items, tents, sleeping bags, and water.

We'd been hiking for two days, and Glacier Lake was visible in the distance. The boys got excited seeing it and picked up their speed. "Mom! We're almost there!" the younger one, Eli, called.

"I know, hon. I see it!" She said, letting him run off in front.

I smiled. Despite the urgency I felt to get back

and see what Ford had thought about the video–and of course, to work things out with him–moments like this were why I led outdoor adventure trips.

I loved feeling like I was an ambassador to the wild. I adored these mountains and loved to share them with people who could appreciate them. Normally, the type of people who booked a multi-day camping trip were the kind who already had a bond with nature and a reverence for the beauty this mountain held. But paying for a private guide meant inside knowledge of the area, plants, and wildlife, which I knew. And we could go at the group's pace, which with two pre-teens, wasn't slow.

We crested a hill, and the boys ran down the other side.

"Someone is there," Laurel, one of the moms said, jerking me from my thoughts.

"What?" My breath caught when I saw the boys talking to a man in army green pants and a black t-shirt.

It was unusual to find other campers up here. In fact, in all my years of making this trek, I never had. That was why I'd insisted Brandon make it one of the offered trips. Still, I had to assume he was friendly. There was a certain camaraderie amongst serious hikers and campers. We looked out for one another.

I scanned the perimeter of the lake but couldn't spot a tent or the rest of his party.

The boys ran on, and he stood looking in our direction as if waiting for us.

I gave a friendly wave as we approached, but even then, something seemed off. The hairs on the back of my neck stood up even though there was nothing threatening about the guy's stance or demeanor. It wasn't until we were close enough to see his face did I realize how fucked we were.

It was Cameron Tully.

From the video. From his Facebook page.

I didn't even know how that was possible, but here he was, standing between a boulder and a clump of columbine, watching my face.

My heart had taken off at a gallop, and my mind raced, but I kept my face smooth. No reason for him to know I recognized him, right?

Except... he must already know. Otherwise, why would he be here? There was no way he could have randomly bumped into me at the Seed n' Feed or the grocery store in town. That would have been plausible. Barely, seeing as this was Sparks, Montana, not a big city. And since the only connection we had was the video and Buck. But up here in the wilderness? We'd driven ten miles out of town to the trailhead and then hiked in from there. We'd abandoned the well used trail the day before. There was absolutely no coincidence.

There was only one way he'd have known where I was. Brandon. How did Tully get out here ahead of us? Oh. He knew where we were headed, not where we were on the trip. So he'd taken a more direct route to beat us to the lake. To ensure he found me. Were there others or was he alone?

I suddenly understood why Ford had wanted to keep me from poking into Buck's death. He'd been right–it was far more dangerous than I'd ever imagined. A murderer had tracked me into the wilderness. And now, it seemed I'd somehow made myself a target.

Time seemed to slow down. The final steps to meet the guy took forever. "Hello," I said politely when we reached him. Sweat ran down between my breasts.

Laurel and Jeanne greeted him as well, having no clue that this was a really, really bad situation. Fuck, I wished we were facing a mountain lion. That would have probably been safer.

"Howdy." He kept his gaze pinned to me.

Fuck.

I needed to protect this family first and foremost. If he came here to kill me, I had to separate myself from them. I could leave them with my GPS, and they could push the emergency button and get through to help. I just had to somehow orchestrate that.

I stopped walking. "You two want to go scout out a good location for our tents?" I asked my clients brightly. "Close to the lake will be great."

"Sure," Laurel said.

I unbuckled the small emergency kit from my larger pack–the one that had the GPS and medical supplies–and handed it to Laurel. "Here, will you take this for me?"

She gave me a strange look as she accepted it, opening her mouth like she was going to ask why, but I interrupted with a curt, "Please?"

She just nodded and left.

"You camped around here?" I made my voice and face cheerful as I faced the man who I'd watched kill another in cold blood. With my brother present.

"Uh huh."

That was it. Creepy as hell.

I'd been trying to tell myself I'd made a mistake.

That this couldn't be Tully, but it clearly was. And I was definitely fucked.

I glanced at his belt and pockets, checking for visible weapons. I didn't see any, but he had a small backpack over his shoulders, and there were bulges in both side pockets that definitely could be a gun or knife. When he saw me looking, an evil smile quirked his lips.

I'd been playing dumb, but the jig was up. My number one priority needed to be separating myself from the family, so they didn't get harmed.

"Are you here for me?" I asked with as much calm as I could muster.

His smile grew larger. "You know who I am?"

I gave a nod. "I think so."

He leaned against a large boulder like we were just two hikers having a casual conversation. "I knew your brother, Indigo. But probably, you know that."

I forced myself to nod. Glancing back toward the lake at the sweet family then in the direction we'd come.

"You have two choices," he offered. "Put up a fight leaving with me, and I kill that family. Or you keep them alive by leaving all nice like."

He grinned, knowing the choices sucked.

"So you can, what? Kill me and make it look like a mountain lion?"

He pretended to think for a moment. "Not a bad idea."

Oh Jesus. He wasn't only here to kill me. He'd have done it by now. And killed the family too. The guy had to be the kind who raped and pillaged while he was at it. But I should've guessed that from watching that video. I presumed he'd been the one torturing the victim before the recording started, and he hadn't hesitated to shoot him.

What was his plan? He'd come to Montana, to this mountainside for me.

I was panicking on the inside. Totally losing my shit. But I had to stay focused. I turned the way I'd led, hoping his focus truly was on me. And only me. Which meant I needed to either lead him off this mountain, or I needed to kill him before he killed me.

The guy was at my flank, not walking by my side. He remained a step behind, so he could watch my moves. About five minutes in, I looked over my shoulder. "Why the mountaintop visit?"

Yeah, it was ballsy to ask, but I needed to know. If he'd wanted me dead, he'd have shot me in the back.

Stabbed me. Whacked me on the head with a tree limb.

I swallowed, freaking at all those possibilities. So far, he'd kept his word about the family. And I didn't have a hole in my back.

"You're the one who treks into the wilderness for a living," he replied. "I only followed."

It made sense that he could've beaten me up here. The six-day excursion involved two nights on Wild Onion Butte to the west, so all he'd had to do was come straight to Glacier Lake to ensure he headed me off before I came back down off the mountain.

My stomach churned, but I forced myself to put one foot in front of the other. I normally did my best thinking while hiking. Hopefully, something would occur to me.

"Why?" The question was so loaded that I wasn't sure what his answer would be.

Why did he kill the Afghan man? Why was Buck there? Why was he here now?

"I came to find out why you were searching my name on your computer."

I tripped over a root and recovered. Ice cold pricked every inch of my skin. How would he have even known that? That had been... three days ago.

Had he been monitoring me?

Of course he had. I had never heard the name Cameron Tully until the video. Hadn't entered it into my computer until after I'd seen it. Which meant he had some kind of trace or something on people searching his name. I'd come up, and my last name was familiar.

That's when an idea occurred to me.

"So I tell you, and then you kill me," I said. I stopped and turned to face him. To see the answer on his face because I couldn't believe anything out of his mouth. "The perfect place, right?"

Adrenaline dumped into my system, and I felt my scalp tingle.

He grinned. He looked more like an insurance salesman from Cleveland than a murderer.

"Tell me what I want to know, and I'll give you a choice. A sad trip off a cliff. A slip into a rushing river. Or a stumble over a tree root where you hit the back of your head on a rock."

I gulped at all the non-suspicious options. I needed to get off this mountain in one piece. If I told him now, he'd kill me and return to the lake and murder the family I'd brought up here too. They'd seen him. Knew I'd left with him.

I ran shaky fingers over my dry lips. Tried to

think. *Think!* Wait. He had only mentioned that I'd searched for his name. Not *where* I'd found it. I might have a bargaining chip.

"I saw a video," I blurted. My hands were slick with cold sweat, and my tongue felt too large in my mouth.

His eyes flared. Yeah, I'd surprised him with that one. *"What video?"* he hissed. His brows slashed down in angry points.

"The one Buck sent me." I tipped my chin up. "Of you shooting Abdul Tareen."

Tully hesitated for a moment, then he said, "Bullshit."

"Buck was translating, you were torturing. A semi-dark room, dirt floor. The man you killed in a dark Afghan uniform." I tried to think of every possible detail of what I'd watched. "Then you ended him with a bullet through the head? Does that ring a bell?"

He scowled at me, and the evil in him registered in my body. This man was more than dangerous. He was deranged. He shook his head, eyes narrowed. "There's no video."

"It was on an SD card–recorded from Buck's bodycam. He mailed it to me three weeks before he died, but I hadn't found it until three nights ago.

Right before I did a search for your name, which was mentioned in the video. Why do you think I recognized your face up there?"

I tipped my head in the direction of the lake.

He narrowed his gaze and studied me. I waited, trying to remain calm. I needed him believing firmly in the existence of the video because it was the only thing keeping me from dying on this mountain. It was the bait I was going to use to lure him off this mountain and hopefully straight to Ford.

"Where's the SD card?"

Bait. Taken.

"Why would I tell you that?"

In a flash, he tackled me to the ground, pinning me beneath his larger body and choking me with both hands at my throat. My backpack had me bowed, and my head canted back. Shit, I should have ditched the stupid thing.

I kicked and writhed, struggling to breathe until I remembered that he needed me alive. Through my panic, I realized he wasn't going to kill me.

I held up my hand, waved it in front of his face in surrender.

Still, he meant to scare the crap out of me because he didn't let go until stars were dancing in front of my eyes. He needed me alive, but whole and healthy was something else entirely.

I sucked in ragged breaths, my body wracked with the fear of death.

I held my hand again, still struggling for breath. "I have it," I wheezed. "I hid it."

He gripped my throat again and used it to pick up my head and bang it back against the dirt. "Hid it where?"

I winced at the sudden burst of pain.

I clawed at his wrists to pull him off my neck. "Wait...hang on," I wheezed.

"I'm listening." His fingers clenched.

"I'll make you a deal."

"No," he said immediately. "Tell me where it is, or you die." He reached for his pocket and produced the pistol I'd suspected was there. He pressed it to the center of my forehead.

I tried but failed to keep the image of Abdul Tareen getting shot out of my mind. I needed to keep it together. I owed it to Buck not to allow this guy to get away with murder again. If I could just lead him down to Ford's place, I knew he and his team would take over. Save the day like they'd been trained to do.

"Hang on!" I said. "Just wait. It's a decent offer. I'll get it for you. We'll go down together. But I want you to leave that family back at the lake in peace, okay? They barely saw you, they're not going to remember anything about you. You and I can just go down the mountain, and I'll give you the SD card. I found it the night before I took this trip, so I didn't have time to show it to anyone or make copies. I just put it in a safe place before I left."

For a second, I thought he was going to accept my plea bargain. He definitely was considering it, but then he shook his head. "No fucking deal. Tell me where the card is, or I will go back and you can watch me shoot that family one by one until you do."

Fuck. Me.

———

FORD

"WHY *THE FUCK* don't we have a helicopter?" I snarled at Kennedy as he, Hayes, and I hit the trail leading in the direction of Glacier Lake. If we had one, we'd have been to the lake within minutes, not after hours of flat-out running. Kennedy had linked Indi's GPS to all of our phones, so we could track her, and I'd sent a text message to it in case she looked but hadn't heard back. The blip showed her at Glacier Lake and hadn't moved since we first pulled it up.

We weren't in the spot where she started from with her group, but another trail that would take us in from the south side. It was more direct, but steeper and would have to use the topo map as a guide. We'd been at a run for over three and half hours, and Hayes kept counseling me to slow our pace, or we'd wear out before we got there.

There was no fucking way. No chance I'd stop running. Not when that killer was out there hunting Indi.

"Helicopter? I will get on it," Kennedy panted from the rear. "Hey," he said. "You need to drink some water."

"No." I kept running, shaking my head as I did. "I'm pushing ahead. You two can pace yourselves if you need to."

The entire time we'd been moving, my brain had assaulted me with images of Buck's last moments. The strain of death on his face when he tried to tell me about the pendant.

"I'd been fucking wrong, Kennedy."

"About which thing?"

He was trying to be flippant, but I couldn't

handle any jokes right now. "You asked me about what Buck said to me before he died. Told me it was probably important. How the fuck did you know?"

"I carry a crystal ball in my pack."

"Seriously. His words make fucking sense now."

While we were hoofing it up a two or three percent grade and we'd been at it for a while, we could still hold a conversation. Thank fuck for being fit. Taft had stayed behind to work with the sheriff's office. His knee couldn't handle this kind of terrain or distance, and I also liked knowing one of the team was handling operations.

"He'd said, *Indi. They can't know.*"

"He meant the necklace," Hayes added. "The people involved can't know she has the memory card."

And now they did.

Buck had warned me about this exact situation, but I'd been too stupid to put it together. Those images blended with the more recent visual of the murder of Abdul Tareen. His swollen and bloody face, the pleading in his voice.

Dread sluiced through my veins, propelling me forward faster. I wasn't going to let the next death I witnessed be Indi's. No fucking way.

Fuck, how could I let this happen?

It took another ninety minutes before I reached the saddle where Glacier Lake hung nestled between two peaks. I'd long left the guys behind, but I trusted they'd be behind me, no matter what. They were fucking SEALs, too.

The GPS signal was coming from a little further ahead. I heard voices in the distance and saw a tent pitched by the lake, so I continued my run until I reached the camp where I found two middle-aged women and two adolescent boys.

"Indi?" I shouted, making enough noise they might have thought I was a bear.

The two women immediately jogged over. "She's not here!" one said as she arrived. "She left with another hiker."

I could tell by the concern on both their faces that they knew something was off.

"She gave us her emergency pack and told us to pitch camp and then never came back."

Her emergency pack. That's where the GPS signal must be coming from.

Double fuck!

Of course. Indi was protecting the family. She left the tracker with them, so they would be found and aided if she didn't return.

"Was this the hiker?" I showed them the image

on my phone I pulled from my pack, even though I already knew the answer.

They nodded.

I took a deep breath and shoved my cell away. It didn't do anything useful up here except show the photo. "Okay. Listen to me–he's wanted for murder, and I believe he came out here to kill her. I have two former Navy SEALs with me en route to this location. I want you to pack up and leave with one of them when they get here. They shouldn't be far behind me."

Panic and fear spread over their faces, and they whipped their heads around searching for the boys. "Oh my God."

"Which direction did Indi go?" I asked.

They both pointed in the direction I'd come, but of course, I hadn't crossed paths with anyone on my way.

Which meant... Indi was leading him off in another direction. Or he was leading her.

Fuck! Please let her still be alive.

"There's a GPS in that pack. If for some reason you have to run–if the perp returns before my men get here–push the emergency button. They'll track you either way but will know you need help immediately. You're going to be okay,"

I added when the panic didn't slip from their faces.

"Wait for the two guys behind me. They'll be here soon and take you out of here."

I retraced my steps, going slower this time, paying attention to the footprints on the ground.

There!

I spotted two sets veering off to the east. I picked up my speed, running as fast as I could without losing the trail. The trail made by my woman and a murderer.

CHAPTER
NINETEEN

INDI

I WAS GOING TO DIE. The hand about my neck gripped so tight it was crushing my trachea. Spots danced in my eyes, and I knew this was it. I had seconds. I wriggled and squirmed, trying to shift. Tully had power and gravity on his side, but I was unstable, like a fucking turtle with my huge pack on my back, I arched sideways and tipped. I wasn't usually two feet wide, but the pack was jammed full, the tent poles wedged in vertically braced my back.

I fell onto my shoulder and hip, Tully's hand slipping away. Coughing and sputtering, I wriggled my arms out of the straps as much as pushed the guy off me. I had a moment to move as he hadn't expected me to fall out of the way. Neither had I.

My maneuvering had me dropping lower, enough so that I was able to bring my knee up. It slid up his thigh and hit his balls. Not full-on, but he groaned and dropped like dead weight.

I panted, gasping, then crying out as I shimmied out from beneath him.

I was sweaty, covered in brambles and grass and dirt as I crawled away then popped to my feet. Glancing over my shoulder, I saw he rolled onto his hands and knees and was panting.

Shit. I hadn't hit him as hard as Steven Hosanski at summer camp in ninth grade when he'd gotten too handsy. Buck had told me what to do, and it had worked like a charm then and maybe now.

I wasn't beneath him any longer. But I was still on a damned mountain. I could run, but as soon as he recovered, he'd chase. Turning around, I took off at a sprint down the slope, aiming for the creek I could see in the distance. Small cottonwoods and shrubs lined it, smartly placed for their roots to absorb the water.

"Indigo!" he shouted after a minute or two, and I knew my head start was up.

I couldn't run like this forever. I was out of breath now. A painful stitch in my side made me wince. Heavy footfall behind me prepped me for his approach. Panic fueled extra adrenaline, which had me pushing harder.

A weight thumped in the pocket of my thin sweatshirt. The temperature had been cool when we'd packed up our tents this morning, and with the thousand-foot gain in altitude, it hadn't warmed up much. Now, I was sweating like I was in a Finnish spa. But the thing in my pocket?

My multipurpose tool I'd had out to pull a hook from a trout's mouth. One of the boys had caught one from the high lake. While he'd wanted to eat it for breakfast, it had been catch and release only, so I'd used the pliers to work the hook free from the fish's mouth before putting him back.

I yanked it from my pocket as I ran, flipping it open into the knife.

"You're a dead woman," Tully shouted as I came to the creek edge. With the steep incline, it had forged deep ravines in the landscape. The deep, heavy rushing water over a nearby waterfall drowned out his fast approach. "You'll see your brother in hell!"

He caught me a second later, and I stumbled. We

fell onto the hard ground. I hit a rock with my shoulder, and he plowed hip first into a boulder at the edge of the ravine.

I gripped the knife and, using every bit of energy I had left, jabbed him with the blade. I felt it hit his stomach then thrust inward.

His hands came up to grab my head, to ram it into the ground, but his eyes widened when his brain caught up that I'd stabbed him.

I screamed when he fell on me again. The wet stickiness of blood poured onto me. Tully's evil gaze bored into mine.

"You bitch," he panted.

I pushed him off again, but this time, he wasn't budging.

It must have been his inward drive to see me dead that pushed him. Gave him his own personal burst of adrenaline.

"If I die, you go with me," he snarled, trying to grab my tool from my hand.

"No!" I screamed, scrambling with him.

"Indi!"

Someone shouted my name.

"Here!" I yelled. "Help!"

"Indi!"

My name came again, and then Ford was there. Was that Ford? Was I dying, or was it really him?

He was wild, panting, frantic. He grabbed Tully and lifted him off me as if he were a rag doll, then threw him onto the ground.

"Indi?" Ford's anxious gaze flicked to me and the blood that covered my shirt.

"I'm okay," I panted.

Ford's attention flicked back to Tully. "You framed David Buchanan. Had him murdered to cover your own tracks."

"Fuck you." Tully was curled into himself, as he tried to get up, hands against his wound. His shirt was covered in blood as well as his fingers.

"You'll die here."

I watched, wide-eyed, as Ford faced off, loomed over Tully, who was trying to crawl backward away from Ford. There was no match.

In this moment, Ford was more mountain man than SEAL. This was his backyard. I was his woman. Tully was going to die.

I knew it solely because we were too far from medical care for the wound I'd inflicted. But Ford wouldn't see the man off the mountain outside of a body bag.

Ford leaned down and pulled Tully up enough to punch him in the face. "That's for Buck."

Tully's head snapped back.

He kicked him in the wound, and Tully shouted in pain.

I shivered at the fierceness of Ford's actions, but I didn't care. That man killed my brother, and he was going to kill me. It had been him or me, and Ford would ensure it wasn't me.

But this man, wounded and bleeding out, had been—based on what Ford said—the mastermind behind the false accusations against Buck. And he'd killed that poor man. He was a murderer. He had no morals. No compass. He was pure evil.

"That was for my woman."

Ford grabbed Tully one last time and hoisted him all the way to his feet. He carried the man to the edge of the ravine, pulled Tully's tortured face close to his. "This is for me."

As if he were throwing a ball, he tossed Tully over the edge, disappearing from my view.

Ford turned to me. I stood, then flung myself at him.

He wrapped his arms around me, held me so tightly I could barely breathe. This time, I didn't care.

"Blue. Fuck."

He set me down and grazed his hands over me, his gaze following. "Are you hurt? Did he—" He stopped talking when he looked at my neck. If it wasn't bruised yet, it surely would be.

"I'll kill him all over again."

I raised my fingers to my throat. It still throbbed where Tully had choked me.

"I'm okay. Oh my God. Ford. I'm so sorry."

He cupped my face and tipped my chin up. "What the fuck are you sorry about? I should have told you everything. Trusted you. I almost lost you because of it."

I shook my head. "No. This happened because of him." I pointed to the ravine. "He... I stabbed him... he... Buck..."

Tears fell then. My adrenaline bled away, and I was weak. Exhausted. Relieved the danger was gone. But... God.

"Shh," Ford murmured, pulling me into his arms again, cupping my head to his chest as I cried. Sobbed.

For Buck. For Ford. For everything that had happened. For being alive and having Ford hold me.

He kissed the top of my head, then tipped my

chin up and kissed my lips. I melted into the contact. The feel of him.

"Buck warned me," Ford said finally, touching his forehead to mine. "Told me to watch out for you. Because of Tully. I just didn't know what he meant when he died. The last thing he said, Blue, was to take care of you."

It was Buck who brought us together at this moment. I knew he'd never have wanted danger to come to Sparks and get me, but here we were. In a way, for a man who wanted us to stay apart, he'd put us together.

"I will," he vowed. "Fuck, for the rest of my life, I'm protecting your sweet ass." He cupped my butt in one hand and pulled me in for another kiss.

I didn't think Buck would like Ford calling my ass sweet, but that was something an older brother would have had to deal with if he'd been here. Because I was going to spend the rest of my life with Ford.

The sound of a helicopter broke through the rushing water. We turned and saw it in the distance. "Search and rescue. It's heading to Glacier Lake."

"Yeah," he agreed. "To collect the people you guided. Hayes and Kennedy are with them. Fuck, we need one of those."

I sniffled and laughed. "A helicopter?"

"Yeah, it's definitely next on my list to buy. I need to be able to get to my woman anytime. Anywhere."

"Ford, that's a *helicopter*."

"Sure is," he said, with a glint in his eye of a man eyeing a shiny sports car. "You up for catching a ride on it? I don't feel like hiking back down the mountain."

He let go of his hold, and I went over to the edge of the ravine. I could only see Tully's leg with all the rocks in the way. The spray from the waterfall soaking his pants. "What about him?"

Ford came over and took the multipurpose tool from my hand. I blinked, not even realizing I still held it. "He slipped and fell."

He didn't say more as he wrapped an arm around my waist and steered me toward the lake. Toward home.

CHAPTER
TWENTY

FORD

THE SEARCH and Rescue helicopter landed at the hospital helipad where Gram, the Buchanans, Brandon, Sheriff Tate, and his deputies Megan and Dan, and Taft all waited for us.

Even though she insisted she wasn't badly hurt, I'd held Indi on my lap for the ride home, needing to feel my woman–alive and breathing–against my body. I'd pressed my lips against her shoulder, her nape, her temple, reassuring myself she was safe. That she was mine.

Tully had touched her. Almost killed her. Bad guys weren't supposed to get to Indi. Ever. My past...

Buck's past, neither were supposed to touch our families. As SEALs, it was our job to keep everyone safe. What every minute of our training was for.

Except I hadn't done it for Indi, and that was going to take a while to reconcile.

Indi had saved herself. Like she'd said, she could handle her own in the wilderness. She'd steered Tully away from the innocent, then gut-stabbed the man. He wouldn't have survived the wound out in the wilderness. She'd have gotten away. I was so fucking proud of her.

Yet I wasn't sure if I'd let her go out in the wilderness without me ever again.

We exited the bird after allowing the outdoor adventure clients to exit first and get shuttled back to town by Brandon. The fucker could deal with that and most likely their request for a refund.

"Indigo!" Page Buchanan rushed forward to claim Indi after I helped her down. Sam hovered nearby, his face ashen and stricken. I was glad she'd changed out of her bloody shirt before her parents saw her, or they would've freaked out. I wasn't sure how they'd gotten the news, whether it was through the gossip grapevine or by Megan or someone else at the sheriff's department. Either way, it had to have been rough. After Buck...

They deserved to be panicky and over-the-top frantic.

To my shock, Sam stepped forward and wrapped me in a man-hug, thumping my back. "You got her out safely, Ford. Thank God."

For some inexplicable reason, my eyes burned. Perhaps with the knowledge that while I may have gotten Indi off the mountain, I'd failed to get their son home to them alive. Perhaps because Sam didn't seem to be holding me responsible for the danger she'd been in to begin with. Either way, I accepted the hug as some small sliver of redemption.

There was evil in the world, and I knew firsthand it touched innocent people. The Buchanans more than most. I wasn't perfect, and it seemed their family didn't expect me to be.

"We can clear Buck's name now, Mr. Buchanan. We have the evidence," I told him, my voice rough with emotion.

Sam nodded. "Taft told me when he explained the situation to the sheriff." He clasped my shoulder. "That was good work."

"No, it was pretty shoddy, actually," I countered. The rotors of the helicopter were slowing now that the engine was shut off. The wind dropped, and so did the noise. "Indi had the evidence the whole time, and Buck had given me the clue, but I didn't put it together. Not until it was almost too late."

Sheriff Tate approached and cleared his throat. "I need to get a report, Ford," he said, tucking his thumbs into his utility belt. In his fifties, he was well respected in the county and had held his elected position for over twenty years.

"Yes, sir. Of course." I stepped aside with the sheriff. Hayes stood by Megan beside her patrol car, apparently giving his story to her. Huh. Were they standing a little closer to each other than necessary? Did he have to reach out and tug on her ponytail?

"I already got the story from your man Taft, but I'd like to hear what happened up on the mountain," the sheriff said.

I debriefed him as succinctly as possible. Quickly, too, because I wanted–no, needed–to get back to Indi. She was safe with her mother, but still. I needed her in my arms. Beneath me.

"He just fell off the cliff?" Tate asked, raising a brow.

I nodded. "Yes, sir. He stumbled right off the edge."

"You didn't help him at all with that?"

I shrugged. "I may have thrown a few punches when I pulled him off Indi."

The sheriff wrote in his notebook. "Self-defense, then."

"Yes, sir." I wasn't going to tell the man Indi had stabbed Tully with her multipurpose tool. She hadn't killed Tully–even though he'd have died from the injury if I hadn't tossed him into a ravine–and I didn't want the thought of that tainting her forever. It was my job to kill–not hers.

"Are you sure he's dead?"

I gave him a look. Did a SEAL know when someone was dead by his hand? "I'm sure," I said. I'd definitely checked. With the angle of his neck, there was no way he'd survived the fall.

"We'll have to send the helicopter back to fish that body out of the ravine," the sheriff said. "Can you show me the location on a map?"

"Absolutely." I pulled out the topo map Brandon had given me and pointed to the approximate location of the body.

When the sheriff was finished with me, I walked over to Taft, Kennedy, and Gram. Gram didn't appear shaken at all. That woman was made of steel. "Good work, Ford. I knew you'd get them all down safely. I'm proud of you. Of all of you."

I stooped to kiss the top of her head. "I love you, Gram."

"I looped in Lincoln while you all were gone," Taft reported. "Kennedy already sent him a copy of the video with a tag to Navy MP. It'll be a fucking nightmare for them, but Buck should be cleared of the murder charge shortly." He frowned. "Not sure if the drug allegations will remain. Kennedy hasn't been able to identify the mystery CO in the video. Yet," he added, confident we'd get it resolved.

I nodded. While we may have cleared Buck of the murder charge, I didn't consider this case resolved. We still had to unearth who was behind the drug trafficking operation and how far up the chain of command it went. Tully may have pulled the trigger in the video, but he wasn't the mastermind. I also wanted to clear my name, not that I cared that much any longer. I didn't give a shit what the Navy thought of me. On paper. I wasn't going back. My life was here in Sparks now. I had Gram, the Buchanans. The Alpha Mountain team was growing. Most importantly, I had Indi.

Speaking of which...

I caught her eye and made my way to her side. An EMT was asking if she needed to be checked out at the hospital.

"Maybe you should, Blue." I wrapped an arm around her and pulled her up against my body.

Her fingers touched her neck and anger set back in. Someone had touched my woman. "No, I'm okay. I just want to go home."

She *was* okay. Perfect. The bruises would fade. If she had nightmares, I'd be there to hold her. Buck could finally rest in peace, and the Buchanans could grieve for their son, the man they'd truly known him to be. And move forward with his untainted memory.

"Okay." I led her away from the others. "May I come, too?" I asked tentatively. While I'd held the shit out of her up on the mountain, we were back in town. Our problems—no, my fuck up—hadn't washed down a swollen creek.

"Yes." Her laugh sounded relieved. "Definitely, yes."

"Good," I rumbled. "Because I have no intention of ever letting you out of my sight again."

She stopped and turned in my arms to face me, her hands sliding up to my chest. I loved her touch. So did my dick although it wasn't the best time for him to perk up and show her. "I don't think that's going to work so well, Ford." Her tone was light and teasing.

"No?" I arched a brow. "Are you opposed to moving in with me in the cabin I'm having built?

Maybe joining our team as a wilderness training expert? Soon it's going to be more than the four of us."

Her eyes shone as she looked up at me. "Hmm. That does sound enticing. Would you believe Brandon turned down my offer to buy the business after he found out I was dating you?"

That asshole. But I focused not on the loser but on the rest of Indi's words.

"Dating? Is that what we're doing?"

"Um..." She rubbed her lips together. "What are we doing?"

"We're moving in together, woman. Or...is marriage on the table? Dammit, Blue, you're mine, and I want everyone to know. So whatever that is, that's what we're doing."

Indi's laugh was low and sultry. She pulled my face down to hers. "That sounds good to me, Ford. All of those things."

I kissed her hard then broke away and blinked. "Did you just agree to marry me?"

She was dusty and dirty but the most beautiful thing I'd ever seen. "Yes? I mean, yes. Definitely. It's always been you, Ford. You were my hero from the day you moved to Sparks. And you still are." She lifted her lips to mine for another kiss.

This time, I went slowly. I moved my lips across hers, savoring the sweetness of the moment. Of her safety. Of having her. Of clearing Buck's name.

When I'd returned to Sparks, I'd never dreamed things would end up like this.

I'd been pissed off and determined and willing to dig in for a long fight. But I'd also been hardened emotionally, and I'd backed away from the Buchanans because my own shame, and my grief made it too painful to see them.

Now, through Indi, I'd plowed through obstacles. Wounds were healing, old and new ones. And I experienced a lightness in my chest I didn't expect to ever feel again. It resembled hope. Love. A future.

It resembled Indigo. My beautiful Blue.

The woman I wanted to spend my entire life with here on the mountain.

CHAPTER
TWENTY-ONE

INDI

FORD INSISTED on carrying me into my house–ridiculous man. He'd been possessive as hell from the moment he found me up on the mountain. Like he needed to keep touching me to make sure I was really okay. Like he was afraid to let me out of his sight.

I wasn't too eager to let him out of mine either.

"I don't need you to prove you're the hero, Ford. I'm already convinced." I laughed when he bumped my feet against the doorframe to get me through it. "Or is this supposed to be a honeymoon carry over the threshold?"

"This is me claiming my woman," he growled, all alpha male.

I stroked his beard and nipped at his neck as he made his way into the bedroom and gently sat me on the bed.

His dark brows furrowed when he surveyed my throat. He lightly traced a fingertip down the side of it. "Does that hurt?"

"A little," I admitted. "But I'm okay. I promise."

His jaw clenched, and his body went taut. "I should get you some ice."

I grabbed a fistful of his shirt to stop him when he turned.

He quirked a concerned look. Oh, my brave alpha hero couldn't fix every problem. He'd learned that–and was maybe still working on it–about Buck's death.

"I just need a shower. And you," I admitted.

His eyes darkened. "How about a shower with me?"

I nodded. Smiled. "You read my mind."

Ford scooped me back into his arms to carry me into the bathroom.

"You're being silly now."

"You won't think I'm silly when I have you pinned against that shower wall screaming my name," he warned, tugging my t-shirt gently over my head.

I couldn't wipe the ridiculous smile from my face. Or stop my pussy from clenching at what he planned. Me, coming? Totally worked. Especially if it was a Ford-induced orgasm.

Ford Ledger was all in with me. It seemed like one of my wildest teenage dreams, only better.

So much better.

Because while I'd suspected Ford was manly by every definition of the word all those years ago, I'd had no idea just how dominant, how possessive, how incredibly virile and powerful he'd be in bed.

I reached for his shirt, and he helped me with a one-armed toss-off of the thing, managing to make it look like porn.

More. I wanted more of Ford. All of him. I wanted to claim him the way he was fully claiming me.

I unbuttoned his pants, but he stilled me with his hands.

My eyes lifted to his in question, but he started rooting through his pockets. Out came a folding knife. His cell. Another knife. A... I had no idea what it was, but the piece of metal probably did someone harm. I couldn't help but laugh at how his pockets were like a Mary Poppins bag of weaponry. He even reached around and pulled a gun from behind his back.

Everything went onto my vanity beside my face lotion and cotton balls. I assumed it was symbolic of what our life would be like together.

When he stopped, he held his hands out letting me know I could continue with removing his pants. I returned to my task, and his grin grew wild and feral like he loved my aggression. He toed off his boots, and I did the same while he pulled my sports bra off–careful not to let it touch my bruised neck.

I pushed his pants down off his hips, and he slid his hands inside mine to cup my bare ass, pulling me up against his body and mating his mouth to mine. We were filthy and smelly, and I didn't care.

"Is this okay?" he asked when we broke apart. "I don't want to be too rough."

"I like you rough." I reached up and cupped his face, loving the silky scratch of his beard. "Seriously, Ford. Be rough."

He boosted me with his forearm beneath my ass and carried me to the shower where he started up the water. I clung to him, my legs wrapped around his waist, my tongue in his ear, needing every bit of Ford.

I realized that until this moment, I'd been holding back. Waiting to see what he'd offer. How much. Whether he'd reject me again or how it would end. I had to admit my upset over him not telling me he was looking into Buck's case had been rooted in fear.

I didn't want to be rejected again, so I'd done the rejecting. Pushed him away before I could hear words from him that could hurt me all over again.

But not now. What had happened on the mountain had made it all become clear. Now I was certain with every fiber of my being that I not only wanted Ford, I was willing to *have* him. To claim him and keep him the way he'd sworn he would do with me.

When the water was warm, Ford stepped in and lowered me to my feet. I stood under the hot spray, so grateful to wash off the dirt of the trail, the terror of the day, and the pain of the past–down the drain with every drop that fell. I moaned at how good it felt.

I closed my eyes and tipped my head back, rinsing my hair. Ford caressed me with soapy hands, stroking over my breasts, under my arms, down my sides. He knelt on the tub floor to wash my legs and feet, then he turned me around and soaped the back of me, taking his time to play with my ass, circling my cheeks, then parting them and sliding his fingertip over my entrance there.

I moaned again into the spray. Shower time with Ford was definitely better than solo. He stood and washed my back, then wrapped his arms around me to play with my breasts. I let my head fall back against his hairy chest, humming softly to the music of the water. I felt his hard-on pressed into my back then squirmed against it.

It was his turn to growl, then he nipped at my neck before grabbing the shampoo bottle and lathering my hair. With gentle hands, he turned me back under the spray of water to rinse off. While I did, he soaped his body clean.

I let him under the spray to wash off while I grabbed the conditioner.

"Uh uh," Ford said when I straightened. "Bend back over, baby. That was too perfect."

I laughed huskily and folded at my hips, offering my ass to him. "Like this?" I asked, glancing at him over my shoulder.

"That's right," he purred, stroking himself from root to tip as he looked at my ass. I was sure he could see all of me. "I'm gonna fuck you just like that." He dragged the head of his cock over my pussy lips. The water washed away my natural lubricant, but the moment he reached around and rubbed my clit, I grew slick enough for him to press in. Arching my back, he slipped in, stretching me around the huge crown of his dick.

Nothing had ever felt so right. After fighting with him, then being away on the trail, then hunted by a murderer, this act felt life affirming.

Me affirming.

Like a return home.

"That feels so good, Ford," I told him as he slid in all the way. He was so big, so thick, and he filled me completely. I clenched, adjusting to his invasion.

"Aw, Blue, I haven't even gotten started." He wrapped a strong arm around my waist to steady me and kept his hips close to mine, thrusting in and up in an intimate, sensual way. "Pleasing you is going to become my life's mission."

I nearly came from that. I definitely wanted to swoon. Maybe sex in the shower wasn't the best idea–I was getting lightheaded from the steam we were producing together.

I splayed my fingers against the tile and braced myself, tipping my hips back to take him even deeper. He slid his fingers back to the apex of my sex to stimulate my clit and a sense of urgency crept over me. My breath quickened, my muscles tensed and released. I rippled around him.

"Please, Ford," I whimpered, right on the edge. Desperate.

"You need to come, Blue?"

I shifted my hips, trying to take more. "Oh my God, yes! Oh, God. *Please.*"

"Me too," he murmured against my ear. "Fuck, this is going to be quick. Next time, I'm going to work you for hours." Instead of separating our bodies so he could pound in harder, he only held me tighter, blending us into one, moving together, one perfect organism. His length filled me, stroking me, kissing me over and over again as the pad of his finger circled and tapped my clit.

It was so much. He was. Us. Everything—

"Please. Oh God, Ford. Please."

"Yeah, baby. You want to go together?"

"Together," I panted. "Please. Let's come together."

His laugh was dark. He thrust into me hard enough to lift my toes from the tub, but it didn't matter because he held me securely. "Let go." He kept thrusting–two times. Three. Five. His movements grew more erratic as he lost control. On the eighth thrust, he shouted a curse. "Now, Blue. Aw, fuck. Come all over my dick."

I did. I came so hard I nearly blacked out. It was the best orgasm of my life, colors swirling behind my closed eyelids. My body tingled, my pussy still clenched with little aftershocks. He remained deep as we caught our breath, and the water started to cool. When it was over, I found myself lifted and carried out of the shower, wrapped in a towel, and gently laid in the center of the bed.

My eyes drifted closed as Ford dried off and laid down beside me. "I love you, Blue. So fucking much." They were the last words I heard before I drifted into the sweetest dreams of my life, wrapped in his arms. Safe.

EPILOGUE

Ford

I HAD her eyes covered as I led her through the snow. It had fallen overnight, and it was crisp and clear now.

"Ford," she complained on a laugh.

Yeah, not much of a complaint.

The cabin was done, and I'd somehow been able to keep her from seeing it. I'd wanted it to be a surprise, and she'd respected that, steering clear of the creek for the past few months. But now it was time to show her where we'd live. Together.

I had paid extra for the contractor to add extra men and build faster. They'd stepped up to the task, and only three months after I'd rescued Indi off the mountain–or she'd rescued herself–it was time for the big reveal.

I'd covered her eyes just before the rise and had guided her the rest of the way in.

I dropped my hands, and she blinked. I stared at her as she stared at our new house. A smile spread quickly across her face. "God, Ford. It's amazing. I love it!"

Relief pumped through my veins, and I smiled too.

I tugged her hand and led her up onto the porch that wrapped all the way around the place. Stomping the early season snow from our feet, I pushed open the glass door.

She looked up and around, then slowly walked around. I followed, but stayed quiet and let her look. A two-story great room with a kitchen. Windows were everywhere. There was a ground floor master and a loft with three bedrooms.

When we got through the entire tour, she flung herself in my arms and kissed me. "It's perfect," she murmured.

I cupped her ass because... well, I always cupped it. It was *my* hand's place to touch her.

"Good, because this is where we're settling."

Her house in town was fine and all, but we belonged here on Ledger land. Not only because it was locked down tighter than a supermax prison, but this was where we'd come together originally and would stay together.

"Buck would be proud, I think," she admitted, nuzzling her nose into my flannel shirt.

I stroked her hair, left long and wild down her back, and lifted her chin.

"His name's been cleared. He died in the line of duty."

Which meant the Buchanans received his death benefits. Money was no consolation for a lost loved one, but it being refused had stung. I wasn't sure what Indi and her parents were going to do with the money, but it didn't matter. Everyone now knew Buck was a hero.

"I'm proud of you," I added.

"For what?"

"Taking over SOA."

She sputtered out a laugh. "Brandon literally left town."

"When you sue him for millions of dollars for unsafe working conditions and–"

She set a hand over my mouth, knowing the asshole only pissed me off every time he came up.

The dumbass wasn't completely stupid because he'd done as I'd said that day and fled. I'd forced Indi–with her parents prodding, too–to seek out a lawyer for how Brandon had spitefully put her in danger by sharing her whereabouts with Tully. The family on Indi's hike had been more than happy to back her in the case against Brandon. He'd settled from Oregon or Arizona or wherever he went.

My woman had the company she wanted and was making changes for the better. Hiring more female guides, setting up women-only trips. Gearing it toward ladies-in-the-wild, which I thought was a fabulous idea.

"I work for you," she said, the reminder soothing me. She told me that often. Pleasing me. I'd told her she should be a consultant for my team. Leading my crew into the backcountry for less wartime-like survival skills. "I think Quincy's going to be a great addition to my guide squad."

We heard the rotors of a helicopter, and Indi rolled her eyes.

"Speaking of," I said.

"I can't believe you actually got a helicopter."

I frowned, but she pressed up onto her toes to kiss me. To make me feel better. I'd always wish I'd had one sooner to save her from Tully.

"And a pilot," I added.

"Quincy's a badass."

Fuck yeah, she was. She'd been in the Navy with my team and extracted us from missions. Her skill behind the stick had saved our bacon more times than I wished to remember. I didn't know a better helicopter pilot. Fortunately for us, Kennedy had heard she'd left the military and was going to take a commercial pilot job. When I'd offered her a better arrangement than working the commuter flights to Des Moines, she'd jumped at the chance.

So now we had a helicopter and a pilot as part of the team. Gram was thrilled to have another woman stay in the house with her and Roscoe.

"Should we get back?" she asked.

"Back? We're home."

Her gaze softened, and her smile warmed my heart and made my balls ache.

I growled, bent down and tossed her over my shoulder.

"Ford!" she squealed, smacking my ass.

"We'll get back to the others after we christen some of these rooms."

I dropped to my knees and lowered her onto her back on the plush bedroom carpet. She reached a hand up and pulled me down for a kiss.

"I'm yours, mountain man."

Yeah, she sure as hell was.

———————

Ready to read more Alpha Mountain?

Continue with Rebel!

Get it now!

NOTE FROM VANESSA & RENEE

Guess what? We've got some bonus content for you with Ford and Indi. Yup, there's more!

Click here to read!

WANT FREE RENEE ROSE BOOKS?

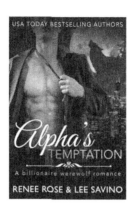

Go to http://subscribepage.com/alphastemp to sign up for Renee Rose's newsletter and receive a free copy of *Alpha's Temptation, Theirs to Protect, Owned by the Marine, Theirs to Punish, The Alpha's Punishment, Disobedience at the Dressmaker's* and *Her Billionaire Boss*. In addition to the free stories, you will also get special pricing, exclusive previews and news of new releases.

GET A FREE VANESSA VALE BOOK!

Join my mailing list to be the first to know of new releases, free books, special prices and other author giveaways.

http://freeromanceread.com

ALSO BY RENEE ROSE

Chicago Bratva

"Prelude" in Black Light: Roulette War

The Director

The Fixer

"Owned" in Black Light: Roulette Rematch

The Enforcer

The Soldier

The Hacker

Vegas Underground Mafia Romance

King of Diamonds

Mafia Daddy

Jack of Spades

Ace of Hearts

Joker's Wild

His Queen of Clubs

Dead Man's Hand

Wild Card

More Mafia Romance

Her Russian Master

Contemporary

Daddy Rules Series

Fire Daddy

Hollywood Daddy

Stepbrother Daddy

Master Me Series

Her Royal Master

Her Russian Master

Her Marine Master

Yes, Doctor

Double Doms Series

Theirs to Punish

Theirs to Protect

Holiday Feel-Good

Scoring with Santa

Saved

Wolf Ridge High Series

Alpha Bully

Alpha Knight

Bad Boy Alphas Series

Alpha's Temptation

Alpha's Danger

Alpha's Prize

Alpha's Challenge

Alpha's Obsession

Alpha's Desire

Alpha's War

Alpha's Mission

Alpha's Bane

Alpha's Secret

Alpha's Prey

Alpha's Sun

Shifter Ops

Alpha's Moon

Alpha's Vow

Alpha's Revenge

Zandian Brides

Night of the Zandians

Bought by the Zandians

Mastered by the Zandians

Zandian Lights

Kept by the Zandian

Claimed by the Zandian

Stolen by the Zandian

Other Sci-Fi

The Hand of Vengeance

Her Alien Masters

Regency

The Darlington Incident

Humbled

The Reddington Scandal

The Westerfield Affair

Pleasing the Colonel

Western

ALSO BY VANESSA VALE

For the most up-to-date listing of my books:

vanessavalebooks.com

All Vanessa Vale titles are available at Apple, Google, Kobo, Barnes & Noble, Amazon and other retailers worldwide.

ABOUT RENEE ROSE

USA TODAY BESTSELLING AUTHOR RENEE ROSE loves a dominant, dirty-talking alpha hero! She's sold over a million copies of steamy romance with varying levels of kink. Her books have been featured in USA Today's *Happily Ever After* and *Popsugar*. Named Eroticon USA's Next Top Erotic Author in 2013, she has also won *Spunky and Sassy's* Favorite Sci-Fi and Anthology author, *The Romance Reviews* Best Historical Romance, and *has* hit the *USA Today* list eight times with her Bad Boy Alpha and Wolf Ranch series, as well as various anthologies.

Please follow her on Tiktok

Renee loves to connect with readers!
www.reneeroseromance.com
reneeroseauthor@gmail.com

ABOUT VANESSA VALE

A USA Today bestseller, Vanessa Vale writes tempting romance with unapologetic bad boys who don't just fall in love, they fall hard. Her 75+ books have sold over one million copies. She lives in the American West where she's always finding inspiration for her next story. While she's not as skilled at social media as her kids, she loves to interact with readers.

Printed in Great Britain
by Amazon